TWISTED TALES TO WARM THE COCK

First Edition

Published by The Nazca Plains Corporation
Las Vegas, Nevada
2013

ISBN: 978-1-61098-334-1
E-Book: 978-161098-335-8

Published by:
The Nazca Plains Corporation ®
4640 Paradise Rd, Suite 141
Las Vegas NV 89109-8000

PUBLISHER'S NOTE
Twisted Tales to Warm the Cock is a work of fiction created wholly
by G.W. Leatherman Parks' imagination. All characters are fictional
and any resemblance to any persons living or deceased is purely by
accident. No portion of this book reflects any real person or events.

Cover, FLESHBLACK
Art Director, Blake Stephens

DEDICATION

To the boys who have been willing to serve this Leatherman.

TWISTED TALES TO WARM THE COCK

First Edition

Erotic Literature by the Black Leather Gloved Hands of
G.W. Leatherman Parks

CONTENTS

ASSAULT IN A DESERTED BUILDING

The Leatherman arrived twenty minutes before the scheduled rendezvous with the boy. He climbed out of the cab of his truck which was parked out of view, retrieved his bag of toys, and sauntered toward the deserted building. The building had been vacant for thirty years or more. It had been vandalized – most of the panes of glass were broken out and graffiti covered the exterior walls. Vines crawled up the side of the building and there appeared to be several saplings growing out of the interior of the building. Looked perfect for the activities that were about to transpire.

He tested the doors, only to find that they were either locked or rusted shut. That didn't present a problem as he cautiously crawled through one of the ground floor windows, careful not to rip his Leathers on the jagged pieces of glass. He marched around the interior, eerily silent. Soon it would be filled with the sound of lashings and cries of pain. Or, at least, he hoped so. He rubbed his spiked cod in anticipation.

He unzipped the toybag and extracted his floggers and paddles. There was an old heating radiator near his chosen spot. He laid them out in order of 'presentation'. Two sets of handcuffs were extracted from his Leather jacket belt. They would provide restraint if he could find a convenient place to manacle the boy. He pulled out his flashlight and was rewarded with two support columns close enough to be utilized. Unsnapping his epaulets, he removed the heavy chain from each side. The key for the padlocks which secured the chains was in his zippered pocket as well as the handcuff keys. He opened them and returned the keys to his pocket.

He next removed two Leather hoods from the bag. He placed the executioner's hood over his own face. The other hood was for the subject. Blindfold and mouthplug were snapped on one side, ready for action.

Lastly, he brought out two candles and lighted them. He placed those on the same radiator, creating a makeshift altar. The only things to be worshipped that evening would be the Leatherman's boots and his cock.

As the Leatherman waited, he pulled a long, black cigar from his cigar case, clipped it and lighted it. Now, all he needed was a subject.

The Leatherman silently upbraided himself for not bringing a watch. He wore his heavy, studded wristbands which matched his cod – no room for his wristwatch. He ran through the rotations he would perform. A smile erupted on his face as he thought of the sadistic pleasures that he was about to enjoy. His cock was already bulging in the cod and he rubbed it appreciatively.

He peered out the windows, but only darkness greeted him. The candles were flickering as a soft breeze rushed through the building.

He continued to drag on his cigar, the glow lighting his face. He hoped that when the boy entered, he would think that he had entered the realm of the devil. Scare him, put him on edge, make him submit more fully – if he didn't turn tail and run.

The boy was in his mid-thirties – had been after the Leatherman on a Leather website to grant him a session. Bearish, good-looking, big muscular arms and a big chest. Nice ass. And what sent the Leatherman over the edge, red fur on his chest with big pink nipples just ripe for the picking. Red beard and mustache. Flat-top haircut. Called himself a biker cowboy. Rode a Harley – his iron horse. From his pictures you could see his veined cock and bullballs hanging to the left in those ass-tight blue jeans. The Leatherman knew he wanted to fuck this boy. Work him over. Squeeze his nips and cock. Fist him. "If he would just arrive," the Leatherman thought as his impatience grew.

The Leatherman continued to gaze out the window, smoking and stroking. Finally, he saw a figure approaching. The boy was marching slowly toward the building. He wore a cowboy hat, bar vest and those damned tight blue jeans. Trying the doors, he entered through the same window and approached the Leatherman.

It was obvious that he was well-trained as he knelt before the Leatherman.

"SIR, good evening, SIR. slave-toy reporting, SIR."

The Leatherman dragged on his cigar before raising the boy's head, removing the boy's hat, and making eye contact with the boy.

"Good boy, you have followed orders well. What is your desire, boy?"

"To serve you, SIR..."

"Good boy," as the Leatherman pulled the boy's head into the studded cod, grinding the spikes into the boy's left cheek.

The Leatherman reviewed the session he had planned for the boy. The boy simply nodded agreement to the terms until the Leatherman said, "Any questions, boy?"

"No, SIR."

"All right, let's get started. Stand up."

As the boy complied, the Leatherman said, "Remove your vest".

In the glow of his cigar light, the Leatherman viewed those tempting tits. He gave them a friendly squeeze. The boy moaned.

"Come over here, boy," the Leatherman ordered as he placed handcuffs on each wrist. The other end of the handcuff was locked and secured to the heavy chain. The chain was padlocked around the column. The same was done to the boy's other wrist.

"Spread your legs, boy." The Leatherman regretted not having a spacer bar, but he couldn't pack up his entire dungeon.

The Leatherman next hooded the boy – it was a shame to hide that handsome mustache and beard, he mused, as he laced the hood into place. Mouthplug snapped in place, blindfold fully in place too.

He stood back. The boy was handsome, restrained in place. His bearish body just in need of a good workover. Ready to receive.

The Leatherman proceeded to administer the first rotation of floggings – lightest to heaviest of floggers. Warming up the boy's back and chest with the varying intensities of the floggers. Of course, he couldn't quite see the results in the reduced lighting, but he knew his marks would be there when he was finished. The boy stood calmly as the first rotation came to an end.

The Leatherman stood nose-to-nose with the boy's hooded face, and complimented the boy. The boy mumbled something, probably a "Thank you, SIR." The Leatherman didn't really fucking care. He returned to his floggers.

Second rotation. Third rotation. Just to warm the boy up.

Extracting a pair of clamps from his bag, he placed them on the boy's nips. The boy flinched as the cold metal bit into his tits. The Leatherman yanked on the connecting chain. The boy's head pitched forward as a healthy yelp escaped from his mouth. The Leatherman simply ignored it.

He yanked on the chain several more times, as he unbuttoned the boy's blue jeans which fell around the boy's cowboy boots.

The boy's healthy cock and balls were at rest, but became excited as the Leatherman massaged them with his gloved hands.

Once again reaching into his bag, the man extracted a Leather parachute and with some difficulty, snapped it into place around the boy's meaty balls. Pulling the chains off his belt which were ordinarily attached to his trucker's wallet, the Leatherman attached them to the parachute. He pulled on them. Surprised the boy. He yelped again. Extracted from the toy bag, wooden clothespins were attached to the loose skin of the boy's cock. As each was attached, the boy sucked in his breath.

The Leatherman hissed into the boy's face, "You likin' it, boy?" The boy's head remained immobile. The Leatherman loudly repeated his question and the boy's head reluctantly shook a slight 'Yes' to the question. "We ain't done yet, boy. Got to fix up that other exit of yours."

The Leatherman pulled out one of the few remaining items in the bag, an inflatable dildo. He greased it up with some lube and jammed it up the boy's ass. It was a beautiful sight – to see that hairy ass with a bigfuck dildo inserted in it. He pumped it up and leaning around to the boy's left ear, "Keep it in there, shithead." The boy's ass clenched shut on the dildo.

With that, the Leatherman began a frontal flogging of the boy. Catching the titclamps with the flogger's tails. Snapping off the clothespins with the same tails. Rattling the parachute's chain. The boy was pulling against the handcuffs but unless he was Samson, there would be no release. After a prolonged flogging session of the boy's front, the Leatherman began assaulting the boy's back and ass. The boy's ass muscles clenched the dildo even as his ass was repeatedly struck with the tails of the heaviest floggers.

The Leatherman was holding his cod as he administered the floggings – his cock was throbbing with sadistic excitement.

The boy's ass was reddening nicely and so was his back as the Leatherman did a momentary examination with his flashlight. He critiqued his work silently. Shoulders need more lashing. Lash underneath and catch the boy's balls. Do a 360 degree flogging. Still a few clothespins remaining as he retrieved several from the floor and reattached them. He pulled on the nipclamps. Once started, the Leatherman could go on for a prolonged period of time. The boy seemed to be all right, taking it with masochistic pride.

The Leatherman removed his Leather glove and put a rubber glove on his right hand. Lubed it up. Removing the dildo by deflating it, the Leatherman inserted first one, then two, then all the fingers of his hand into the boy's hole. The boy apparently had his hole stretched on previous occasions because the fist went in easily. Right up to the wrist. The Leatherman explored and prodded. His hard-on was now raging. The boy's back was arching, his ass maneuvering to take more of the arm of the Leatherman. Right up to the spiked wrist gauntlet. When the boy's ass felt the spikes, he tightened his asscheeks.

"Oh, no, boy, don't close that shaft down now. This miner wants to explore," the Leatherman instructed and with that the Leatherman drove the spikes into the boy's hole. Several dozen spikes assaulted the boy's ass and the boy wrenched forward. The Leatherman had to stop playing with his own cod, to wrap his free arm around the boy's waist and pull the boy's ass back toward the spikes. The boy was protesting.

The Leatherman yelled, "You muthafucker… take it." and continued his assault on the boy's rectum. It felt so damned good, sliding those spikes against the boy's ass. His fist continued to penetrate the boy's ass. And his hard-on continued to throb.

Just then, he heard a door slam – in the distance, but still it caused him to retract his fist and position his gloved hand over the boy's plugged mouth. He hissed in the boy's ear, "Don't you make a sound, boy…" He quickly extinguished the candles.

It was obvious that two people had entered the building somewhere to the east of the flogging site.

A man's voice was barking orders, but the Leatherman still could not quite make out the conversation that was being held. Scuffling and struggling could be heard. Heavy footfalls and what appeared to be wrestling. The rattle of heavy chains. The strike of a match. Evil laughter. Muffled groans.

The Leatherman stood silently as did his captive.

What seemed to be an eternity went by, before he heard the distinct sounds of Leather straps against human flesh. The Leatherman had heard those same sounds often enough in his own dungeon.

"Fuck," he thought, "another scene is going down...."

With two floggers attached to his belt, the Leatherman quietly followed the continued lashings and the moans emitted from what appeared to be another slaveboy. It was just too much to resist exploration.

There were a number of twists and turns in the building, but, as he rounded a corner he witnessed two men. One was tied between two columns, just like his sub. The man was wearing tan breeches and tall, black boots.

The other man, the flogger, was wearing a tan uniform, the distinctive patrol uniform of a CHiPs cop – tan shirt, tan breeches and black, high boots. Motorcycle helmet.

The flogging patrolman was growling at his victim, "Take it pussy boy, you're a cop, you can take it."

The other man was already covered in red marks, revealed by a lantern, positioned near the boy's shoulders and hanging from a nail embedded in the column.

He flinched as the flogging cop continued the barrage of floggings.

The Leatherman's cock was excited at the scene – two sadomasochistic cops playing rough. It was too much for him to remain silent.

He marched up silently behind the cop and said loudly, "Let me help you, Officer."

"What the fuuccckk?" the cop exclaimed as he spun around and viewed a hooded man in full black Leather. He raised his flogger, but the Leatherman caught it with his powerful arm.

"Just want to help you in your training of this pussy ass."

The cop sputtered, "I work alone. Who the fuck are you? You know you're trespassing…"

"What the fuck?" the Leatherman replied, "So the fuck are you and you're beating a fucking cop."

The cop reached for his holster, but the Leatherman, anticipating such an action, slammed his body against the cop's hip, trapping the cop's hand and holster.

"You're interfering with police business…." the cop snarled.

"Yeah, right," the Leatherman snorted, as he raised his flogger from his belt and whipped the restrained boy's back. The boy flinched at the strength of the flogging – pitching forward.

Despite his outrage at the intrusion, the cop nodded his head and remarked, "Nice."

"I gotta boy in another section of the building. Let's tag team, show these muthafuckers we mean business." He extended his gloved hand and the two sadists shook hands.

Positioning themselves to the left and to the right, the two men began an extended flogging of the boy's back. Welts and soon, streaks of blood began appearing on the subject's back. A cop bulge and a similar bulge in the Leatherman's cod were very apparent.

"Can't get enough of this, bro…" said the cop.

"Then we're two twisted fuckers, because I can't either."

Pretty soon, they had the boy's breeches down around his boots and were lashing his ass. Both would flick between the legs and catch the boy's cock and balls. He wrenched forward every time a Leather tail struck his privates. The boy was breathing heavily.

The cop marched around to the front and lifted the boy's head, making eye contact. He spit in the boy's face. "Now you got two Captains to worry about, boy."

The Leatherman followed the cop, encircling the boy's neck with his gloved hand. "And whipping ain't all we're gonna do to you…" The two laughed as they returned to flog the boy's ass and back some more.

"You say you have a boy here?" the cop asked.

"Yeah, let's let your pussy boy cool down…"

The two marched back to the Leatherman's restrained boy. He was attempting to pull the restraints away from the column. Heavy streams of sweat were running down his muscular chest.

"Nice," the cop commented as he pulled on the boy's dick. The boy's meat had softened, but soon became hard with the touch of the cop's Leather gloves.

The cop reviewed the boy, remarking, "Nice piece of ass," as he slapped it several times.

"Yeah, I was examining his hole when I heard you arrive."

"Oh, well, let me show you how a cop does that procedure." He marched back around and kneed the boy in the solar plexus. The boy doubled over as far as he could. The cop moved swiftly to the boy's ass and plunged his gloved hand up the boy's hole.

The boy was screaming inside his hood.

"Damn, you must have gone for special training for that maneuver," the Leatherman remarked as they both laughed. The cop continued to explore the boy's hole. He roughly pulled his fist out and unsnapping his nightstick, began twisting the nightstick into the boy's hole.

"Damn," thought the Leatherman, "gotta get one of those…"

The boy was twisting and flinching, as the wooden manrod inched its way up his rectum. The cop had a satisfied smile on his face as he extracted the nightstick. He unzipped his breeches, lubed his cock with his own spit, and jammed it up the boy's shaft.

He pumped rapidly and was rewarded with thick cords of cum, some of it spilling out of the boy's ass and onto the floor.

The Leatherman had been massaging his already swollen dick. As soon as the cop pulled his hard flesh nightstick out of the boy, the Leatherman inserted his. He planted his manseed in the boy's hole as well.

The boy was moaning and heaving from the rigorous session.

"Let's top your boy off," the Leatherman suggested as they returned to the restrained cop and performed the same scene.

The sky was beginning to lighten as the two finished their assault on the cop. The sadists were both exhausted from the sessions, mansweat covering their bodies.

"That was fucking great, bro." the cop said, "Let's rendezvous next week."

"Deal, bro," as the two embraced. They each untied their boy and went their separate ways, only to return the following week. And the week after that...

If you are anxious to explore a deserted building, first check the perimeter of the building. If you see a cop car and a truck, you better hightail it out of there unless you want to be the next victim. My cop buddy and I are always looking for fresh ass to plow.

FATHERLY DESIRES

The sadistic Leatherman led the submissive down three flights of steps, turning several times to urge the sub on.

"We must hurry, we don't have much time...." he snapped.

He was taking off his outer layer of clothing as he rushed down the steps. As he reached the bottom step, he hastily removed the last vestiges of his clothes to reveal a Leather harness, a studded cod, and knee-high boots. His wrists were covered with studded gauntlets, his hands with tight Damascus gloves.

"In," he ordered, as he pushed the sub into a small, sequestered chamber with a newly-constructed St. Andrew's cross and a bench.

"Disrobe, sub," as he proceeded to lace an executioner's hood over his own face.

The boy was soon naked except for boots.

He pulled the sub toward the cross and quickly placed the boy's wrists in bondage cuffs. He hooded the boy's face.

"Now, we're ready…" the Leatherman impatiently said as he extracted a clipped cigar from the pouch on the bench. He lighted it as he picked up his first flogger.

Background music already started, would disguise the flogger's strikes as he began the slow rotation.

The boy was not a novice, but despite that, flinched at the first strikes.

As the strikes became more pronounced, the boy began responding with groans.

"Shut up!" the Leatherman ordered, but as he struck with more ferocity, the boy's groans became louder and turned to yelps.

The Leatherman stopped briefly, to buckle a plug in the boy's mouth.

The background music was gaining strength and the Leatherman knew that he could continue his floggings with little interruption or discovery.

He pulled his second flogger off the paneled wall near the bench.

He stood back and let loose with a cruel barrage of strikes. The sub's body twisted and turned, but the flogger always found its mark.

An evil smile slowly appeared on the Leatherman's face as he continued. His cock had quickly reacted to the scene. The boy's cock was shriveled from fright and his butt cheeks were tightly clenched. The Leatherman had plans for that to change too.

Strikes from the braided flogger caught the boy's back and arms, armpits, ribcage, and ass until there was a delicious crisscrossing of marks.

The background music rose in pitch and the Leatherman knew that this was a good time to introduce the sub's ass to his studded butt paddle.

It struck twenty-five times, causing the boy to wince and attempt to pull away from the strikes.

The Leatherman's gloved hand held the paddle with two hands as he delivered the last ten, with all the frustrations of the day centered in them.

The sub was breathing heavily as the Leatherman stopped the assault. Yet another flogger found its way to his sadistic hands and the flogging on the boy's naked flesh continued.

The next flogger that he selected would test a sub's mettle for continuing. It had tips that resembled barbed wire and would produce a pronounced sting and draw blood.

The background music rose once again in volume, making the Leatherman realize that it was the perfect time for him to subject the sub to the 'tenderizer'. It had the desired effect as droplets of blood appeared on the boy's back. The boy moaned and twisted. It just caused the Leatherman's cock to throb in its pouch, seeking release from its Leather enclosure and seeking a warm hole.

The Leatherman finished the flogging and approached the boy. He spit on his gloved hand as he placed his hardened rod against the boy's tightly-clenched asscheeks.

With his right hand, he covered the boy's nostrils, whispering to the boy, "Open your cheeks for me or else I'll use that flogger until your cock is raw…"

The boy slowly unclenched and a man's hard rod made its way up the sub's tunnel.

The music continued and was nearing crescendo.

The Leatherman rammed his cock into the boy's hole and furiously pumped his cock back and forth. The cock's manjuices were gathering at the base of the shaft and were quickly making their way to the cock's head.

He held the boy's hips as he pumped his cock in and out. The boy moaned as the cock invaded his rectum. The music swelled as the cock inched further up the invaded hole.

The Leatherman was pumping vigorously as his cum shot out of his cock and up the sub's private territory. The seed came and came, some of it spurting out of the boy's ass and falling on the floor.

The last passage of music was beginning and the Leatherman quickly wiped his cum-slathered cock on a fuckrag taken off the bench.

He released the cuffs and unlaced the sub's hood.

"Get dressed quickly!" the Leatherman yelled as he himself began re-dressing.

The boy was slow to move for which he received a slap on the face, "I said hurry, boy."

He led the way up the steps and darted into a bathroom at the top of the second flight of steps. He pulled the sub in after him.

"Check your clothing and see that everything is in place."

He led the sub up the final flight of steps, emerging into the church's apse.

The cross had just been carried up the aisle as the Father and the newly-hired assistant priest fell into place. The church service began a few minutes later. As the Father continued the service, he could feel trickles of blood running down his back from the flogging he had just received at the hands of his new Master.

GREAT UNCLE PETER'S TRUNK

I have been a Leatherman for more than half of my life. Proud of it. Comfortable with it. Never questioned it.

Sometimes though, in innocent ramblings, where in the hell did it come from?

I grew up in comfortable surroundings in New Jersey. My parents were not drugged-up hippies or free-thinking Communists. Good, solid people. I'm sure they never anticipated me growing into a sadistic Leatherman. And I followed the route they wanted me to follow. College, Grad School. I'm very comfortable in my intelligence – have been successful in my career. Just no wife and no grandchildren. Just a flogger-wielding Leatherman who likes to take young men into his dungeon and have them submit to me.

But, what strand of DNA bore the S&M gene, tell me? Never saw my Father raise his hand to my Mother or my siblings… or me.

Never really had an answer until a week or so ago.

My great grandparents had immigrated to the country, arriving at Ellis Island. Left Germany and started a life in New Jersey. Their children were grown by the time they immigrated. My paternal grandfather came with them, however, as a young man of 23. Married here. Children born here. 'Normal' by all standards.

Grandfather always talked about the 'old country'. His desire to go back and see his sister and brother who had remained in Germany. He never made it. They corresponded regularly – at least he and his sister. His sister died five or six years later. His brother – they lost contact except for a Christmas card. Signed 'Peter'. Never any correspondence to indicate how he was doing in the 'old country'.

When Grandpa died, my Father took up the torch and corresponded with Uncle Peter. And when Dad died, I carried on the tradition.

The Christmas card would always arrive a few days before Christmas.

I began writing longer and longer letters to Great Uncle Peter. Questioning about the family. I was interested. Maybe I'd make a trip someday – but you know how that goes… work, vacations to PTown, San Francisco, instead of a wholesome family visit.

"Michael," Uncle Peter wrote last Christmas, "I am not well. I fear that I will not live to see another full year. I am sending you some items which may be of interest to your research."

I had forgotten about his promise of the items when, in March, the delivery service left a substantial box on my back porch. The return address was indeed that of Great Uncle Peter.

It sat in my hallway for several weeks before I had the time to open it.

It was an old trunk, with Leather straps firmly holding the contents inside. It didn't look very exciting and I anticipated that it would hold letters from my family to Great Uncle Peter. Maybe obituaries, graduation cards and wedding announcements, personal mementoes.

That was as far as I got for another week or so. Seemed I had a lot of appointments with handsome submissives and I wasn't going to interrupt those pleasures for a musty old trunk. I carried it upstairs and put it in my library.

I had quite forgotten it when a card arrived from Great Uncle Peter's attorney. He had passed away and left me a small inheritance, along with his other nieces and nephews. I regretted that I had not sent him a thank you for the trunk and its contents.

Even though I was Leathered up and anticipating the arrival of a new conquest, I trudged upstairs and undid the straps. Opening it, there were the expected letters, tied carefully in bundles. Yellowing newspaper clippings. A knock on my door prompted me to close the trunk and greet my latest boy.

Even though he was nervous, the boy was a good subject. I escorted him to the dungeon, restrained him, and did my usual flogging rotations on him. His back and ass were covered in red lash marks before too long and my cock was bulging. He was a handsome boy. A little meat on his bones, very nice ass.

I turned him around, hooded him and subjected him to forced smoke and cock-whipping with a delicious flogger meant for that purpose. The boy moaned and rolled his head from side to side as the flogger tickled his cock and balls. My cock continued to harden as I saw the boy flinch. Damn, it was so exhilarating.

The session lasted longer than I thought it would and so, I bedded the boy down in my pup cage. I wanted to work this boy over some more. And I did, with my morning coffee. Slept in Leather that night. Woke with a spectacular hard-on. Extracting the boy from the cage, I had him take my morning piss and then shot my seed in his mouth. Down to the dungeon for several more sessions. For the last session, I strapped him to my fucking bench and fisted him, followed by a very intense assfucking. My cock was very happy as I spilled my seed in his hole.

After twenty-four hours, I released the boy. We had a total of four sessions – all of them taking him a little further each time. For a boy so nervous at first, he really rallied. The boy left and I cleaned up the dungeon.

Several days later, I was bored. Had no boy lined up for the weekend and so, I once again opened the trunk. Rifling through more of the same from the last investigation. Toward the bottom of the trunk was a small grouping of letters written in Germanic script. They were addressed to Great Uncle Peter from someone named Hans Mueller. I was never a linguist and so, I put them aside. Next out of the trunk were old snapshots. Most of them were groupings of people, smiling broadly into the camera. And, of course, most of them had nothing written on the back. One stood out however.

Two young men, with Nazi swastika armbands, stood with their arms around each other. My cock perked up as I viewed the uniforms, especially the knee-high, spit-shined boots. And Leather gauntlets. My cock rose even further. Long black cigars in each of their hands. Just so happened I was wearing my black Leather uniform with my shined Dehners as I rubbed my cockbulge. As I turned the photograph over, I was rewarded with the penned inscription, "Peter & Hans, Poznan, 1943. The day of Herr Himmler's speech."

I took the letters to a friend of mine who majored in German in college. Told him I would pay him for the translations. Finally, two weeks later, Tom called and said that he had the translations for me.

We met for coffee. Tom looked slightly nervous as he handed me the pack of letters and his computerized notes.

"So, what did you find? I know that my Great Uncle was a Nazi soldier…"

"That's only a small part of it, Michael."

"What?" I questioned.

"You really want to know?'

Mind you, Tom knew nothing of my proclivities. He was happily married with wifey and the kids.

"Well, out with it," I insisted, as I took a long swig of coffee.

"Peter and Hans were apparently... er, lovers. Forbidden during the Nazi regime."

"Oh," as I sucked in a long breath. I knew Peter had never married, but didn't expect to hear that news. Thought I was the only black (Leather) sheep. I thought instantly of the photograph and my cock rose in my jeans.

"Yes, and, uh... experimented with... how shall I say, unorthodox activities..."

"What do you mean, were they playing with sheep?" I said, as I tried to suppress a grin.

"No, um, male to male... um, activities. It's all there... you can read it for yourself." He handed me the sheaf of papers and excused himself.

I would try to soothe him later, but was anxious to read the transcriptions for myself. I finished my coffee and hastened back to my house.

The letters reveal a relationship no one in the family ever spoke about. Maybe no one knew.

In the earliest dated letter, Hans indicated that he very much enjoyed their night together. Sitting out under the stars, groping one another. But the relationship had quickly darkened and by his third letter, he wrote, "Master, I very much enjoyed the session you had planned for me and you in your attic. The fondling and groping. However, I did not expect your belt to come off your breeches and be whipped by it. My ass still bears the marks." His letters continue as the relationship continued to evolve into a Master-slave relationship. At one point, Hans was terrified what their Kommandant would say when he saw that Peter had shaved the slave's head, in fact his whole body. "Master if the Kommandant's aide does an inspection for lice, it will reveal my pubis shaved. I fear reprisal." Acceptance came at some point, although it is not clear when.

He began signing the letters, "Your obedient and most unworthy slave hans." It was apparent that Great Uncle Peter whipped the boy in ever increasing intensity and numbers. "Your unworthy slave deserved the 400 lashes you gave it. I cower to say it, but your riding crop is an instrument of evil, Master."

He wrote twice about Uncle Peter's 'Circle Parties' in 1945. I had an idea what they meant but in the second letter it becomes clear that Uncle Peter was sharing his handsome slave with his fellow Nazis who were similarly inclined. Apparently, the slave would position himself naked in the middle of Uncle Peter and three friends. They were all dressed in full uniform (which made my cock bulge) and they would march around in the circle, taking strikes at the boy's naked flesh with their riding crops. The men would be smoking and drinking and getting naturally high from the floggings they were inflicting on Hans. He wrote the day after the second session, "The beatings still hurt; I am covered with red lash marks on my legs, ass, chest, and arms." But, at the conclusion of the letter, he wrote, "Thank you, Master. I know I deserved them as your property. It is your will that I follow." That was the last letter chronologically.

And so, my answer came at the conclusion of reading the translations. At least, one that had plagued me for some time. I now knew where my sadistic tendencies came from. It was a strain of genes within my family. I was suddenly provoked at myself for not writing Great Uncle Peter before he died. I wanted more. What happened to Hans and Peter after the War?

In doing some research, I did find that Great Uncle Peter was tried for War Crimes, but he was ultimately acquitted. He resumed life in the village from which my family had come. Did Hans remain with him after the War, serving Peter as his slave? In searching on the internet, I did find a Hans Mueller still living in a nearby village. Was it him? I penned a letter and anxiously looked in my mailbox each day for a reply in that (what was now) familiar Germanic script. A month went by, and I felt certain that he had probably died and perhaps he and Peter were playing in Leather Heaven or Leather Hell – wherever. As LeatherMaster and slave.

As I am writing this down, I am seated on my back porch. A typical day of leisure for me. Full Leather. My soft Leather breeches caressing my thighs, the cod holding my cock, and my spit shined boots reaching to my knees. Muir Cap. Nazi armbands. Can't help it, it's my heritage. I hold no racist thoughts. Just enjoy the image of powerful men in black Leather. It is raining heavily. I'm dragging on a big black cigar.

I am surprised as a car pulls down my long driveway. Hmm, I don't remember an appointment with a boy.

A man in a raincoat and a fedora gets out of the car and walks slowly up on the porch.

I get up to greet him as I view a handsome face with a white mustache.

"Yes?" I inquire.

"Lord and Master, I am Hans, once your Great Uncle Peter's slave."

I was in shock as he pulled off the raincoat and despite his age, revealed a firm, masculine body in Leather cod pants and knee high boots.

He fell to his knees and kissed the tip of my boots. "I have come to serve you as my new Master."

HALLOWE'EN — WHAT A DRAG!

Hallowe'en has never been one of my favorite holidays. I'll say that right from the start. However, a Hallowe'en Party was scheduled the night before the monthly meeting of our Leather Club at our home bar and it was strongly suggested that Club members attend. I was reluctant to go. I have never considered my Leather a costume, it is my lifestyle. And no, you don't have to wear Leather that evening; you can be Superman, the Easter bunny or go in drag. I have never been into drag and never intend to. I have a dick between my legs and I am proud of it.

So, I suited up in cowboy gear, with Leather fringed chaps, a Leather fringed jacket and a Leather cowboy hat. That's as close as I come to a Hallowe'en costume. When I arrived at the bar, I was surely the most unimaginative of the Club members. I didn't give a fuck. I grabbed my beer and selected my place against the wall, propped my booted foot against the wall, and watched as the Club members trickled in.

A couple of Club members went all out – one guy is a florist and in my mind, had spent too much time on his costume.

He was dressed as a scarecrow. He had done a really good job – a stuffed crow rested on his shoulder. Give him the prize and move on.

I had been there about two hours and had talked to a couple of the patrons. But, no chemistry. My dick didn't even twitch that familiar twitch when there is someone whose ass I wanted to fuck. I kept thinking, "Come on, Road Captain, arrive and count us present, so I can fucking leave." I'd rather be home watching a porn flick.

The night progressed and the Road Captain had not yet appeared. Probably humping a boy at home – the lucky fuck.

A rush of people came in – presumably they had been to a private party and were now making the circuit. Several twinks filtered in – their half-naked bodies clothed as Cupid, a baby, and some 'alien' with his naked chest painted green, gold circles around his nips. None of them interested me. Give me a boy with a little meat on his bones.

One was a drag queen that caught my eye, however. He was almost tasteful in his appearance – or was it a woman? Too far away to tell. 'She' wore a big picture hat and a long purple gown, tightly cinched at the waist. Opera-length gloves. The makeup was not gaudy. And a handsome face. Hmmm, must be a woman. No interest. I turned away to watch the other exit of the bar in case a single boy was exiting to the back alley, looking for a man to suck. My cowboy cock needed it.

I turned back around only to find the 'purple' woman standing next to me.

"Would you have a light, Mister Leather Cowboy?" she said in a sweet Southern accent.

Never one to be impolite to anyone, I reached in the pocket of my chaps and extracted my lighter. I held the lighter while her gloved hand held her cigarette.

"Thank you ever so kindly," she responded.

"You're welcome... Ma'am," as I tipped my hat.

"I am new in town and heard that this bar was filled with gentlemen who treated ladies kindly," she said, as she batted her eyes slightly.

"Well, Ma'am... you do realize you're in a Leather bar, where the men have interests other than women," I replied, playing along with her game.

"Oh, mercy," she replied, fanning her face with a lace fan which had been dangling from her wrist, "I had no idea." She blathered on, attempting to convince me that she was an innocent.

My temper flared – I was not interested in coupling with a drag queen, no matter how attractive. "Come on, cut the crap, you're a guy in drag."

"My boyfriend likes me like this... do you?"

"I have to say, that you are damned attractive as a woman, but I like men to be men," I answered, realizing that she was stimulating my southern regions.

"Hmmm," she replied, her gloved hand reaching down and slowly stroking the Leather pouch which contained my mancock.

"Seems you must have an interest in me or else your rocket wouldn't be firing, ready for lift off. I do enjoy pleasuring men of Leather," she said, as she squeezed it hard.

I squirmed as my cock indeed was hardening.

"I'm Tess, by the way..." she whispered as she stuck her tongue in my ear.

"I'm...G.W.," I managed to say as her tongue continued to moisten my ear.

"I wonder if she gives blow jobs?" I thought, as my mind began to race. 'Her' portrayal was so convincing, but not over the top like so many drag queens.

"Would you let me buy you the drink of your choice, so we can chat some more?" she coyly asked. Before I had a chance to answer, she was over to the bar, buying a beer for me and a drink for herself.

I offered to pay for the drinks, but she refused, "No, Sir, I feel very comfortable with you" as she moved a little closer to me, her thigh rubbing my cock through its Leather pouch.

We continued to talk, and my cock was becoming more aroused. I had to find a boy to relieve me soon! Enough of this shit and nonsense, I was not attracted to women!

She continued to flirt until I finally excused myself and told the bartender to tell the Road Captain I had been here, and left.

On the drive home, I kept replaying the scene in my head. 'She' was damned attractive – had one of those personalities that made you feel glad you were a man – but, I'm a man – a Leatherman. Damnit. I like to fuck men. Not women. Not even drag queens. I insisted my boys appear in Leather when we had a session. Fuck, was I turning soft? Would I start dressing in fishnet stockings and heels? Never. I enjoyed my masculinity too much.

But fuck if I didn't dream about her. She was down on her knees, the picture hat bobbing up and down as she sucked me off. I exploded in her mouth and could see the stains of red lipstick on my cockshaft. Thankfully, I woke and there were no lipstick stains on my dick, but quite a lot of dried cum on my cock and bed sheets.

The next day was our regular Club meeting. Attendance was mandatory. I suited up in my usual cycle Leathers and headed out in my truck. I attempted to put the episode out of my mind as I journeyed to the bar. My cod was extended with an over-anxious cock. I tried to concentrate on a muscle boy I had played with only the week before. His ass was the only pussy I needed. And he had given me a great blow job. But, just as quickly, I envisioned Tess on her knees, sucking me. Damn, what was happening to me? I parked my truck and with some difficulty, walked to the bar, a fully-extended rod in my cod.

The Club members filtered in. I was usually the only man in full black Leather. Some wore their bar vests, a couple of the guys had their cycle jackets on, but most were complaining it was unseasonably warm and wore tee shirts and shorts. So be it. I wear my Leather every day.

We discussed Club business. Tonight was prospective member's night for the Club and there were four being considered. Again, Club attendance was mandatory. Except for the Road Captain, who apparently never did show up the night before. His partner, the President, made excuses for both of them. Mandatory, except for the select few who were above the rules. It wasn't long after that I was kicked out of the Club for non-attendance. Who the fuck cares? I ripped my back patch off my colors vest and sent it back to them. An insignia doesn't make me a Leatherman.

The meeting concluded and the Club members went off in their little cliques. My buddy Gene and I went out for dinner. He was the only other guy that afternoon in full Leather. We respected one another for that.

Later, of course, we returned to the bar and like the night before, I retrieved my beer and took my place against the wall. Guys started filtering in. I sucked on my beer and cigar (at this time, you could still light up in a bar), watching the guys come in. I was nursing my second beer, when a nice-looking guy came in. A pup. A cub. Clean-shaven. Compact. Leather head-to-toe. Good looking cycle jacket and fitted Leather pants. Asstight. Gloves. Boots. He looked around somewhat apprehensively, but retrieved a beer and headed for a spot on the wall next to me.

I nodded and he smiled.

"I'm G.W., a member of the Club, welcome to our bar."

"How do you do, Sir, I'm Gregory."

"First time here, son?"

"No, Sir, I was here last night."

I thought hard, but didn't remember seeing this attractive pup. But the bar was crowded and I had left prematurely, disturbed at my cock's behavior.

"I've put my application in for membership in the Club. Don't know anybody... so, I'm glad to meet you," he said somewhat tentatively.

"Well, you'll enjoy it," I said, as I lied a little. I didn't want him to feel uncomfortable.

We talked for a long time – he visibly relaxed as I talked about some of our Club activities, my own Leatherhood.

I really liked this boy. Down-to-earth, polite, intelligent.

We continued to talk until the President of the Club banged a beer bottle on the bar and made motions for members of the Club to congregate in the back room to meet the candidates.

Gregory, of course, was one of the four.

"Who is sponsoring Gregory?" When no one raised their hand, I raised my gloved hand and told the Club the little I knew of Gregory. It was apparent that the Club liked what they saw as he was voted in along with the other three.

With that formality over, Gregory and I resumed our conversation.

We went out in the alley where I drew him toward me and began fondling his Leathered asscheeks.

In return, his upper thigh began massaging my cod which was already reacting to the young man in front of me.

"You are a good-looking pup, Gregory."

"Thank you, Sir."

"I pulled his head toward mine and we kissed. He continued to rub my cod, the contents of which had enlarged considerably. My gloved hands were rubbing his crotch area, his back, his arms, locking my arms around him and feeling that ol' familiar man urge.

I really wanted to take it further – he had on those damned pants which have a zipper for access to his ass. Damn, if I didn't want to finger his hole. We were in a public place and two guys had filtered out from the bar into the alley and were watching us intently.

"As I pulled his head closer to my Leathered chest, I suggested strongly that I wanted him to come back to my place.

So, we could continue the exploration. I'm no prude and I've been known to pull my cock out in the play area of a bar, but I wanted this boy all to myself. No audience.

With my gloved hand firmly around his neck, I led him through the bar and out onto the street. We retrieved my truck (his vehicle would be safe until the next day) and we drove back to my lair. I could not keep my right hand off of him. Fondling his leg. Squeezing his crotch. Brushing his cheek. He took my gloved hand in his mouth and sucked each finger. My cock was at full attention as we drove into my driveway.

As I turned off the truck's lights, I pushed his head down into my crotch. I just couldn't wait another fucking minute. I unsnapped my cod and let him nuzzle my cock. He knew what to do after that and I soon jacked off in his mouth. He swabbed my cock clean and then we finally exited the truck.

I was hornier than hell for the boy. Got him inside and plastered him against the wall of the hallway. Rubbing my Leathered body against his. Urgent kissing. I reached under his jacket and rolled his tits between my fingers. I was fucking totally aroused. My cock was already pulsing. I was gripping his jaw with my gloved hands and had thrust my tongue in his handsome mouth. My cock pressed into his crotch area and it was evident that his Leather Master was exciting him.

We took a momentary break to head upstairs. On the bed, I was all over that handsome boy. Our Leathers uniting. Our cocks hard and pulsating against their Leather enclosures. I could not stop grinding my body into his. He was just so fucking sexy, alluring, handsome. Pants were soon open and our cocks were pressed bone-to-bone.

In all honesty, it did not take long to jack off. Didn't think my cum production could work that fast, but it sure as hell did. Cords of jism covered his cock and mine. Our manseed and boyseed combined.

We continued for a long time – man and boy intertwined in passionate Leathersex. No stop to it. I felt like a fucking machine. Wanted to pump it down his throat, up his ass, all over his cock. The boy was just so receptive to all that we did, with me in charge.

We fucked non-stop. Both of us covered in sweat and cum. I just could not keep my hands off the boy. As the sun peered through my bedroom window, I rolled off of him and we lay for a while, breathing heavily.

He was the first to recover. He crawled to the end of the bed and repositioned his left cheek on my cock. It was soon aroused as the boy did a slow tonguing of my cock head and shaft.

The boy was insatiable, a quality I admire. I fondled his head and pushed it down when he came up for air.

Despite predictions that there was no cum left in my cock, he found it – must have drawn it from a reserve in my fucking ears or someplace…

My bone responded. His handsome mouth fully engulfing my manrod. I viewed the look of pleasure on his face. Beads of sweat on his forehead. He sucked my bone dry. .

After sucking me dry, I pulled him toward me and he laid his head on my chest.

"Daddy…" he started.

"Yes, son, what is it?"

"I have a confession.…"

'Oh, Shit,' I thought, 'here it comes – what's it going to be?'

"The other night…"

"Last night, boy?"

"No, two nights ago… I was in the bar and couldn't take my eyes off of you."

"You mean at the Hallowe'en party?"

"Yes, Sir"

"Hmmm… I sure don't remember seeing you, pup," as I wrapped my arm around his neck.

"Well, I was in costume… as Tess." There – his revelation was out. Fuck! How could I have not known!

"Well…," I started, as I fumbled for words, "you make a convincing woman. But, pup; when you become my boy you're never gonna wear it again…"

"Your boy? Are you serious…? Sir?"

"Never more serious, son." I examined his lips closely to make sure there were no traces of red lipstick and then I drew him to me and we kissed for a very long time.

At that moment, Tess ceased to exist, although I still have memories of that night in the bar when I almost crossed the line.

A Boner Book

SINS OF THE FATHERS

Samuel Cockerham rushed to his grandfather's estate in Winchester. He had been living the life of a profligate in London until word reached him by post that his grandfather was gravely ill and was not expected to last the week.

"The old gaseous fart," Samuel mused as the coach made its way through the pitted roads of the countryside, "it's probably just a clever ruse to upbraid me for dropping out of school." It was true. Samuel had dropped out – he had absolutely no interest in learning a profession. What he wanted was to have his cock sucked by a male prostitute. To tweak the nips and slap the arse of a willing young man. One that Samuel could bugger during the night and then dismiss like discarded rubbish the next morning. Toss a crown at the departing whoreboy.

Yes, Samuel was not interested in anything except circulating among the riff raff of society, astounding the whores with who he was, and jamming his superior cock up their arses. Samuel was next in line of succession. When the old fart died, Samuel would be named the 13th Lord of Coddington, inheriting his grandfather's substantial estate. All at the tender age of twenty-three, it seemed.

"Oh, I guess the old man could attempt to disinherit me," smugly thought Samuel, "but then the line would come to an end…" Of course, Samuel had no intentions of marrying. The thought of lying in bed with a woman, even of high birth, reviled him.

The coach rocked and swayed as it seemingly hit every depression in the dirt road. The carriage ride was already into its second day and Samuel was bored with the endless bucolic scenery. "Damn, wish I had hired Jack Robbins to come along." Jack was a favored 'companion', used to Samuel's arrogance and mistreatment. But Jack liked the jingle of the crowns in his pocket from the several nights he had spent pleasuring Mr. Samuel. 'Oh, yes, indeed,' Jack often thought, "Young Samuel is my ticket to fortune if I play my cards right and pleasure him just so. And so what if he strikes my arse with a riding crop once in a while. It surely got worse treatment from my ol' man."

Late in the afternoon of the second day the coach arrived at Coddington Manor. Samuel stirred and climbed down out of the coach to be greeted by the family retainer, John.

"How is he?" Samuel asked.

"Not well, Master Samuel. He is not long for this world," John sighed.

"Well, guess, I better go in before his eyes roll back into his head and Lucifer carries him away…."

"Master Samuel, it is not good to speak of your grandfather in such a disrespectful manner!"

Samuel got right into John's face and exclaimed, "Say anything like that again and you'll be pushing a peddler's cart in London."

John hung his head, "I'm sorry, Master Samuel, I meant no disrespect."

"Get my trunk and don't be slow about it," the young man snapped as he headed to the front door.

He mounted the staircase, two steps at a time. His grandfather's bedroom was down the hall and to the left. The room was heavily curtained, but Samuel could make out the dim outline of his grandfather in bed. His breaths were coming in ragged rasps.

Samuel removed his grey Leather gloves as he approached the bed.

He took his grandfather's hand which was cold, but twitching as if Grandfather was having a bad dream.

Samuel roughly shook his grandfather, announcing, "Grandfather, it is Samuel, your grandson."

"Yes, Samuel... I know... it is... you. I knew you were... ar...riving," the old man said with difficulty.

"What is it you want, Grandfather?" Samuel said, impatience apparent in his voice.

"As you... may realize, Sam...u...el, I... am not... long... for... for this... life."

"God!" Samuel thought, "I feel like I am in a badly-acted play... To think that I am missing the moist lips of Jack on my rod for this..." Samuel's thoughts evaporated as he realized his grandfather was talking about his inheritance.

"What was that, Grandfather?" Samuel politely said, suddenly more interested in what the old man had to say.

"I said... Samuel... soon you... will succeed... succeed me as... the Lord of... Codding...ton. You... must... carry this... title... with dig...nit...y and... honor." The old man was gasping between each syllable. Samuel tilted the old man's head upward and slopped some water down his throat. It merely set the old man off into a coughing fit.

When the coughing subsided, the old man began speaking again. "Your father... was a... good man... it was a... sad day... when... we lost... him. You... you... were only fifteen... and be...fore that... Marg...Marg...," continued the old man, as he began to sputter.

"Yes, yes, Margaret, my mother, died when I was eight... get on with it!" Samuel said, a little too sharply.

"She... died...giving birth... to Hen...ry... your... brother..."

"Yes, I know, Henry died a few days later..."

"Our...fam...ily... has been... plagued... with... misfor...tune. I...was... appointed... as your guardian," continued the old man, who seemed to finally have garnered some strength to talk without sputtering and stammering. "I attempted to raise you... in the best possible...way. Giving you ev'ry advan...tage life has to offer." His speech was interrupted by another coughing spell.

Samuel rose from the bed and stared out the window until the coughing stopped.

"You, Samuel," began his Grandfather, "have not taken... best advantage of my gene...ros...ity... How...ever, Samuel... you are my heir...named...in my... will and... testa...ment. You shall inherit... my estate. Lord Cod...ding...ton..." The old man fell silent.

Samuel's head was already spinning. The eventuality had finally arrived. He immediately thought of the parties he would have – filled with sumptuous foods, fine wines and spirits imported from London, Portugal, France, and of course, tasty male flesh... all to do his bidding. Oh, it was heady for the young man.

His grandfather now had his eyes closed. He was breathing heavily. But he was still breathing.

"Damn, get on with it, old man," Samuel silently thought, "Go to meet your maker." Samuel briefly pondered the idea of placing the feather pillow over the old man's face, but thought better of it. Natural causes would catch up soon enough. In the meantime, Samuel needed to purchase a few new things for his lair. "And just where do I find someone like Jack Robbins in this desolate hole?" Samuel wondered, wishing for the pleasures of Jack Robbins.

Samuel descended the staircase and rang for John. John appeared and was ordered to have the stableman saddle a horse. The future Lord was headed to the nearest town some twenty miles away.

"But, Master Samuel, Lord Coddington requires you to be here."

"Nothing I can do for him, John. Now, do as I say!" Samuel snapped.

Samuel rode out to the town center. It wasn't much to speak of, but hopefully would supply the future Lord's immediate needs.

He first stopped at the small spirits store which was good for a couple of bottles of Jamaican rum and Spanish wine. The shop contained a small collection of pipe tobaccos and treasured cigars, imported from Cuba. Samuel grabbed up a box of the cigars. His purchases were inserted in the saddlebags.

His next stop was at the shop of John Brittingham, the local tailor.

Samuel interrupted the tailor in the middle of a fitting for a local who was being measured for a new clawhammer coat in Merino wool.

The tailor excused himself to deal with the abrupt appearance of the brash young man.

"Yes, Sir, what can I do for you?" Brittingham politely said.

"I need a new suit of clothing as soon as possible. I will soon inherit the title of Lord of Coddington Manor"

"Oh, why Sir, you must be Lord Coddington's grandson. I had heard that you would be arriving."

Without ceremony, Samuel replied, "Yes, he will soon be dead and I will assume ownership of the manor."

"Why, yes Sir, we have some very fine Merino wool, which would make a most excellent suit. As you can see and feel, it is the finest."

"I'm not interested. I want my breeches to be of the finest lambskin Leather. White. The jacket, also of lambskin, to be dyed blue, with gold buttons."

"Well, yes Sir. I can accommodate. It would take several weeks for me to order the hides from London, but I can have the outfit made for you in two weeks after the tanned skins arrival."

"Is that the best you can do, tailor?" Samuel impatiently replied.

"Well, yes Sir, unless I was to go to London myself."

"Very good. Do that, tailor. Leave tomorrow."

"But Sir…," Brittngham replied.

"Measure me…now," Samuel said firmly.

Brittingham made his apologies to the customer who was provoked at the intrusion, but after Brittingham assured him that he would soon finish the fitting and offered the man a glass of claret, Brittingham returned to Samuel with his tape measure and a scrap of paper.

"Stand up on the block, please Sir." Brittingham requested of the future Lord.

"Stirrups, Sir?" Brittingham inquired.

"Yes, tailor, I want all to see exactly what I have to offer," Samuel replied, not caring if he offended the sensitivities of the tailor or his customer.

"Certainly, Sir," Brittingham replied as he ran the tape measure up the inseam of the young man's leg. The stirrups would effectively keep the breeches tight and reveal his cockbulge.

"I want it tight around the buttocks area too," the arrogant young man ordered.

"Yes, Sir," replied the tailor.

Samuel removed his shirt, revealing his muscular chest. "Make the jacket tight."

The specifications for the outfit went on as the tailor took very careful measurements. The other customer had drained his glass of claret and waited impatiently.

Samuel ignored the man's sighs. After all, he was more important than the man. He was the new Lord Coddington.

"Sir, do you need boots to complete your outfit? I also am a cobbler by profession as you can see." A cobbler's bench with boots to be repaired was stacked near the back of the shop. Scraps of Leather, mostly brown and black, were scattered on the windowsill.

"No, I am wearing a fine pair I had made in London. As you should have noticed when you measured me," Samuel retorted.

The measurements complete, Samuel threw a handful of gold coins on the counter.

"Send for me when you have it complete, tailor."

"Yes, Sir," Brittingham replied as the young man drew on his tight, grey Leather gloves and exited.

"Well, that was certainly a spectacle," the provoked customer replied, "Surely the demise of the House of Coddington."

"I fear so, Sir," Brittingham replied as he returned to the measurements for the merino wool coat.

Lord Coddington breathed his last three days later. Without ceremony, Samuel had him buried in the local churchyard. He didn't give a tinker's damn whether or not the townspeople mourned the loss of his grandfather. Notes of sympathy were discarded without reading them. Upon his return from the burial, in fact, Samuel began making plans to stock the estate with a retinue of young men, whore boys, for his constant pleasure. He reasoned, however, that they should be of the middle class, not London whore boys. He wasn't sure where to look. He wondered aimlessly around the estate for several days, refusing to see the townspeople who had stopped by to offer their expressions of sympathy. John insisted that a black mourning wreath be placed on the door, but Samuel just as quickly stripped it away, not wishing anyone else to come to the door.

On Tuesday afternoon, Samuel was restless. He had settled in the the library for a treasured cigar and several glasses of rum. He was idly paging through several of his grandfather's books when John interrupted him.

"Yes, what is it?" Samuel impatiently remarked, not bothering to look up from the book he was perusing.

"Lord Fullerton is here to see you."

"What does he want?"

"To pay his respects, of course, Sir." Samuel was about to tell John to send the man away when the man made his appearance in the doorway. Samuel could not help but stare.

The man was an imposing figure, in full military uniform. And he was handsome.

Samuel could not help but stare at the man's cockbulge which was quite evident in his tight military breeches. His bucket boots rose to the knee, spit shined to a mirrored finish.

"Yes, yes…" sputtered Samuel as he quickly rose, "Come in, Sir." John was dismissed and the door was closed as he left.

"Thank you. I apologize for the intrusion, Lord Coddington. I have arrived too late to pay my respects to your grandfather, who was a valued friend of my family."

Samuel felt as if he had lost the power of speech as his eyes lingered upon the handsome face of Fullerton. He was a man of about forty, with just a touch of grey at the temples. His green eyes danced as he talked to the smitten Samuel.

"Come in, come in, please… let me offer you a glass of rum… and a cigar."

"Gladly," Fullerton replied as he sat in the chair vacated by Samuel.

Samuel drew up a chair to be nearer his guest. The man sat with his legs spread evenly apart. His manhood was clearly visible in the tight breeches. It was obvious that he was muscled underneath his military jacket. Powerful hands. At ease with his masculinity.

Fullerton slowly rotated his cigar to get an even draw as Samuel offered a lighted match for the purpose.

"You have arrived lately from London, I understand. You were here when the Lord passed away…."

"Yes, Lord Fullerton, I was with him at the end after a long life of service to his family and his country."

"Admirable of you," Lord Fullerton said, with a strong note of skepticism in his voice.

"And what are your plans for Coddington Manor?" Lord Fullerton inquired.

"I suppose I shall lead the life of a country gentleman."

"Admirable," Lord Fullerton said once again, his voice once again heavy with doubt.

"Perhaps you should visit Fullerton Manor at your convenience. I can provide some guidance toward your desires." The Lord casually massaged his crotch area with his gloved hand.

Samuel licked his lips nervously.

"How so, Sir?"

"Well, a handsome young buck like you... surely has carnal desires that need to be satisfied. And now that you are wealthy, every young firefly in the county will be offering his services to you."

Samuel was sweating. He could feel the heat of passion rising in his crotch.

Fullerton continued talking but Samuel was not comprehending what Fullerton was saying. He wanted those full lips on his, the man's tongue exploring the inner recesses of his mouth. He wanted to be pressed against Fullerton's body – their two poles side by side.

He had never been tongue-tied in his life – always arrogant, self-assured, knowing and getting what he wanted.

Fullerton's hand rested on his manhood – it was outlined in the tight breeches.

"Sir," Fullerton interrupted Samuel's train of thought, "I really must be going – I have an appointment coming..." Fullerton smiled slowly, as he held his crotch area, "and some things just cannot wait."

"Yes, yes, of course, Lord Fullerton. A pleasure...."

As Fullerton exited the room, Samuel's eyes reviewed the handsome ass tightly outlined in the military breeches.

"Do take me up on my offer, Lord Coddington," Fullerton commented as he swung around and caught the direction of Samuel's eyes, "I meant it sincerely." And with that, he was gone.

Samuel could do nothing – his member had swollen and was dripping in his breeches. He retreated to the chair where Fullerton had sat. Within a few minutes, his cock exploded with his man juices. He played the scene over and over in his mind. He imagined the two men fondling and kissing, in tight breeches, and then naked, slamming their bodies against one another's.

Three days later, a handwritten invitation arrived, addressed to "Samuel Cockerham, Lord Coddington. Personal."

Samuel ripped the envelope open, to read, "Harrison Compton, Lord Fullerton invites you to a private party, Saturday, 17 January 1817. Manly Pleasures Disguised as Frolic."

Samuel began sweating and nervously pacing. "What does the invitation mean exactly?" Samuel pondered. He finally concluded that it must be a masked event. His imagination roamed. Possibly whore boys available for male pleasuring. And since the party was surely to include important people such as himself, they should wear a disguise, masking their identity.

He called for John, "Have the stableman saddle my horse. I must hasten to the town center."

Samuel mounted the horse as soon as the horse was equipped to ride and flew toward Brittingham, the tailor's shop.

He pushed the door open only to find Brittingham at his table near the window.

"Oh, good morning, Lord Coddington. I trust you are well after the emotional turn of events..." Brittingham started.

"Yes, yes... how is my outfit progressing?"

"As you can see, Sir, I am sewing on the buttons as we speak." Brittingham held up the jacket as evidence.

"Oh... fine. How are my breeches?"

"Ready for you to try on, Sir."

Samuel hastily pulled off his boots and slipped off the breeches he wore. He pulled on the tight, white Leather breeches.

It was apparent that Brittingham was an excellent tailor as they fit superbly. Samuel admired himself in the looking glass. He smiled as he pulled them a little tighter, revealing his extended manhood. "This will stir Lord Fullerton's man juices," Samuel silently mused.

"Excellent, tailor. Let me try on the jacket," Samuel said as he pulled the jacket out of the tailor's hands.

Once again Samuel admired himself in the looking glass.

He returned the jacket to the tailor and remarked, "I need one more thing…"

"Yes, Sir, I have just enough to create that…"

The tailor once more took measurements and after accepting another pocketful of gold, promised that the item would be ready by Saturday morning, in time for Lord Fullerton's party. The tailor thought it an unusual request, but he never questioned his clients' needs.

Samuel dressed carefully Saturday afternoon, pulling on his tight breeches, his handsome jacket, his spit-shined boots. He placed the item in his saddlebag. He would add it before knocking on Lord Fullerton's door.

The afternoon dragged on as Samuel nervously paced the room. Finally, checking the mantel clock every few minutes, it was time for him to depart.

He rode recklessly over the roads which connected his estate to that of Lord Fullerton's. He thought of the night he would spend in the arms of Lord Fullerton – kissing, fondling. He might even consent to go down on the tasty cock of Lord Fullerton if Fullerton would reciprocate. After buggering Fullerton's whore boys.

A young, handsome man greeted him and took the reins for his horse. Samuel jammed his riding crop in the top of his boot.

"One moment, boy," as Samuel extracted a black Leather hood from his saddlebags.

"Lace this in the back, boy," Samuel said.

With the black hood in place, he marched to the door.

Another handsome young man answered the door – he was clad in black Leather cod breeches. He was shirtless.

"Good evening, Sir. You are Lord Coddington, the Master is expecting you."

Samuel's eyes darted from side-to-side as he scanned the well-appointed hallway.

"Lord Fullerton awaits you, downstairs."

Samuel hastened down the steps, only to find a dimly-lit hallway, lighted with candle sconces.

"Well, young Samuel, I see that you have risen to the occasion as I knew you would," Lord Fullerton's voice said playfully. He appeared at the end of the hallway, He wore black Leather gauntlets and black Leather cod breeches. He too was hooded with a black Leather hood. His handsome, muscular chest was shirtless. He carried a length of black Leather and a riding crop in his left hand.

Samuel licked his lips nervously as he approached the Lord.

Without ceremony, Lord Fullerton pushed him to the floor and guided Samuel's head to Fullerton's bulging cod.

"Wait, I don't understand…," Samuel sputtered.

"You will in good time, boy." Fullerton said with authority, as he held Samuel's head in place with his Leather-covered hands.

"You are going to pleasure me…" Fullerton remarked, without emotion.

"What about the other guests?"

Fullerton just laughed, replying, "There are no other guests. Tonight, I am your Master and you will pleasure me," as Fullerton grabbed for the unsuspecting boy's wrists and held them firmly until he had them tightly bound with the length of Leather.

"Now get up and follow me or I shall drag you to my pleasuring room."

Samuel struggled but Lord Fullerton merely laughed as he manhandled the boy.

Samuel was soon tied to a wooden cross. Lord Fullerton had removed Samuel's new jacket and thrown it on the dirt floor. A triangular piece of Leather, retrieved from a nearby table, was roughly stuffed in Samuel's mouth.

Samuel struggled even more as the first cracks of Lord Fullerton's riding crop laid open his back with bloody welts. Lord Fullerton was laughing at the predicament his young victim was in.

He stopped momentarily, to whisper harshly in Samuel's ear, "How do you like the private party so far, boy?"

Samuel started cursing at the Lord, but with the gag in his mouth, he could only stutter and stammer.

Once Lord Fullerton was satisfied with the marks on Samuel's back, he reached around and unbuttoned Samuel's breeches. They fell around his knees and whipping on his buttocks commenced.

Samuel twisted in his Leather bondage straps. They had been tied tightly and were cutting into his wrists. He began crying.

The tears went unnoticed by Lord Fullerton who massaged his swollen cock within his breeches.

Abruptly, the whipping stopped. The fragrance of a Cuban cigar permeated the room.

Lord Fullerton was viewing the boy from a distance as he released his large cock from its enclosure.

Spitting on it and massaging the shaft, he marched over to Samuel and without ceremony, thrust his manpole up the boy's ass.

Samuel cried out once more, but in an odd way, he felt pleasure. His hole began to relax as the cock eased up his chute.

Lord Fullerton was thrusting his pole with swiftness. In and out, in and out – inching further along each time.

Samuel began to duplicate the rhythm of the thrusts as Lord Fullerton reached around and pulled on the boy's unsuspecting nipples.

Lord Fullerton began to moan as his cockjuices began to rise in his cockshaft and up to the meaty head.

Samuel's head reared back, his arms tensed as Lord Fullerton slammed his masculine body into Samuel's body.

Fullerton let out a mighty roar as his cock released his cream up Samuel's chute. Some spilled out on to the floor.

Fullerton remained in place for some time, as he squeezed and pinched Samuel's nips. He released the right nipple and squeezed Samuel's manhood. It was fully erect and throbbing. With just a few squeezes of the gloved hand, his cock exploded with white cream against the wooden cross and the wall supporting it.

Samuel slumped against the wall. Fullerton wiped his spent cock with his gloved hand and placed the fingers in Samuel's mouth. The boy eagerly licked the cockjuices off of it.

"Good boy," Fullerton remarked as he struck the sore ass of the boy with the riding crop.

"Now, let's do it again," Fullerton taunted as he began whipping the bloody back of the boy, "You'll get used to it, boy. Your grandfather told me you would be a good subject, just like your father was."

SPIKES OF FEAR

By all accounts, I'm a pretty mean fucker. I don't take any shit from the boys who serve me. And I have scared off more than a few before they even show up. And I have to admit, I admire the boys who do have the courage to show up – after all, they don't know what they are in for. My dungeon is set up for the pleasures of S&M. And by God, you better be ready for it. I'm here to have fun and to pleasure my own cock with a sub's ass and mouth.

When I was more active in the bar scene, it was never enough for me to wear a bar vest. I wore full top Leather – make no mistake, I'm cruising for a sturdy boy who can take my forms of discipline. Be prepared for it. Have some experience in being whipped, CBT, dildo play, fisting, et al. No fucking nonsense. Got no time for it. Don't fuck around with me.

I found that the tougher you look, the real boys step up. The pussy boys stay behind. Fine by me.

I was out cruising one night, actually was just out for a Leather walk. It was a balmy night and I was in full man-fucking

Leather. My favorite spiked cod carried my over-anxious cock. Had the cod custom-made. And it looks intimating – wanted it to be. The spikes could leave a few marks on any boy's ass. Wanted it to. I had added spikes on the epaulets of my jacket and of course, wore several chains on each arm. Might need them to lead a boy to a secluded place.

Smoking a big cigar. My mirrored sunglasses in place, even though it was way past dark. Muir cap pulled low over my forehead.

Turned the corner and headed down my favorite 'meat-packing' alley. Hustlers a plenty, but hell, little scrawny dudes thinking they could pleasure me. I sneered at them and moved on.

Two or three business guys were getting blow jobs in doorways. They looked at me only briefly and lowered their eyes. Wasn't interested in them anyway. I was looking for someone exceptional, someone to get my cock more aroused than it already was. Couldn't help but stop and look at my mirrored reflection in a shop window. Muir cap pulled low. Harness underneath my jacket. Spit-shined boots to the knee. Nice, tight ass.

Marching on, I saw a handsome Leatherman standing under a streetlight, leaning against it. Fuck, my cock was pointing like a fucking divining rod. He was in head-to-toe Leather. A similar spiked cod.

I was eyeballing him from behind my mirrored sunglasses. He was probably doing the same. However, he wore a full Leather hood, with spikes resembling a Mohawk haircut. That hood was fucking awesome.

I sauntered up to him, "How ya doing, bro?"

"I'm doing fine, Sir," he replied.

"What brings you out tonight?"

"Well, Sir, probably the same as you," he said. The two "SIRS" had not gone unnoticed.

I closed the gap between us and reached for that spiked cod. His dick was nice and hard.

"Umm," I suggested, "I'm looking for an exceptional hookup, and you look like you might be interested in the same…"

He nodded his head and bowed it slightly.

It was then that I noticed the hood had a belted closure around the neck, with rings. They were partially hidden by the collar of his jacket.

Without further word, I unhooked one of the chains from my epaulet, and attached it to one of the rings.

"Come with me, boy," I ordered, as I yanked on the chain leash. He followed me with no resistance.

He followed me obediently back to my place. And said nothing as I manacled him to the St. Andrew's. I crushed my body into his, feeling those spiked cods – mine pressing into his cod and his pressing into mine. For me, it was instant arousal. I could feel his cock harden. I ground those spikes into his cod and felt the electricity develop between the two of us.

I unzipped his jacket, unbuttoned his shirt and was rewarded with two handsome nips, enlarged through many play sessions. Nip rings, just like in my nips. Tattoos over both nips.

I couldn't keep my gloved fingers off those nips. They hardened just like his dick. I squeezed and pulled and twisted. The boy had his eyes closed, but was moaning quietly. My cod pressed into his crotch even more urgently as I pulled his head toward mine and our tongues found each other's. It was urgent, primeval, animalistic.

I reached down and pulled my cod down, my manrod escaping. I then pulled his cod off, to be rewarded with a throbbing boy rod. I held the cocks firmly in my gloved hand as I began rubbing them, squeezing, pulling.

Our mouths were locked together as he moaned. I sensed that he was begging to shoot. Ordinarily, I would have denied a boy's request to cum, but I wanted to feel our cumjuices combine, slathering cords of jism together, making this boy and me one.

I increased the rubbing and pulling. I could feel our cock shafts throbbing. Cum collected in the shaft ready to explode through the piss slit.

We continued to kiss. Both of us were sweating and moaning.

One final stroke and we both exploded. Cumjuice on our Leathers, landing on our boots. And we continued kissing until we had exhausted our mutual supplies of cum.

I was sweating profusely and he was heaving as I unmanacled him and forced him down on the floor of the dungeon.

"Lick it off my boots and pants, boy."

Those tasks accomplished, he remained on the ground until I pulled him back up by his leash.

I rubbed his hooded head. "Good boy."

After that night, I accepted phillippe as my boyslave in training. He had been with several Masters before, but needed a refresher course in Master-slave relations. He got his ass whipped on more than one occasion. But that boy was exceptional.

After six months, I felt that phillippe was well-trained. We had gone to a number of Leatherparties, with me leading him on his leash. He had done well as my boyslave and I wanted to show him off. We had gone to the Leather bars and I had shown him off to the Masters in attendance.

He was well-educated to treat the Masters with the respect they deserved. Down on all fours, licking their boots. Taking the Masters' cigar ash.

I'd allow a certain amount of groping, but that boy was mine. He was not allowed to address a Master unless I was present. I allowed him to converse with his fellow boys, but most of the time, his mouth was plugged and that handsome spiked hood was in place. The Masters were curious about his face but no one was allowed to view it for the months that followed.

We were walking home from the Leather bar one night. I was leading slave on his leash. It was late – after 2 AM.

We turned down the darkened street and I viewed two handsome hustlers conversing under a streetlight. Their asses were packed in faded jeans, outlined in chaps. Tight tee shirts revealed their muscular arms, both banded with tribal tats.

I pulled the leash up short and whispered to my slave, "I want to get into their pants, slave. You're going to assist me." With that I took the leash off his collar and stowed it in my back pocket.

I approached the two young men who were now aware of my presence. They apparently thought I wanted to pass and stepped aside. Instead, I stopped and dragged on my cigar for a minute.

"Gentlemen, how are you this evening?"

"Just fine, Sirs, and how are you tonight?" one of them said, with a slight trembling in his voice. I'm sure we looked intimidating. Both in full head-to-toe heavy Leather. I had on my executioner's hood. I had recently added spikes in a Mohawk pattern, similar to phillippe's hood. phillippe had on his 'Mohawk' hood. Spikes on our epaulets. Chains dripping off our epaulets. Spiked boot chains. Simply put, we looked like the non-nonsense fuckers we were.

They apparently took my boy as a top, just what I wanted them to do. He stood silently by.

"Looking for a little rough action," I responded.

"Uhm, what kind of rough action, Sir?"

"My partner and I would like to work your asses over," I responded, as I massaged my already-excited crotch.

The two looked at each other, a bead of sweat appearing on the forehead of the taller of the two.

Before they had a chance to respond, I motioned for them to stand against the nearby wall. Some reluctance on their part caused me to grab each of them by the neck and escort them to the wall. They stood motionless although trickles of sweat were cascading down their faces. A silent communication with phillippe caused him to stand right behind the shorter of the two as I assumed the same position behind the other.

I reached around and unsnapped the chaps and unbuttoned the tight jeans of the boy on the left. His pants fell to his knees, revealing a handsome ass and an equally handsome cock. phillippe followed my lead.

I had carried a small butt paddle on my D ring and pulling it off, lightly paddled the two creamy asses. The boys moaned, arching their backs and spreading their hands against the wall. I repeated the paddling, handing off the paddle to phillippe who proceeded to give the boys a number of paddlings.

My cock was enlarging as I was delivering the paddlings. In between rotations, I massaged it. I reached over and grabbed phillippe's cod which instantly hardened at his Master's touch.

I unsnapped my cod and my cock sprang forth. I spit on it to lubricate it and eased it up the boy's hole. I nodded for phillippe to do the same. He unsnapped his cod and massaged his dick – a rare opportunity for him to touch his cock. Ordinarily, he was not allowed to play with his cock – it was my property.

He too spit on his cock and eased it up the other boy's hole. Through the hood's eye slits, I could see that his eyes were twinkling. Usually the recipient of a butt fuck, he was enjoying this new sensation of power.

The boys were moaning as our cocks slid up their chutes. I began pumping slowly, deliberately. phillippe was banging the boy and I touched his shoulder, indicating with my hand that he should slow the action down, prolong it.

In and out our cocks slid up the lubricated holes. Once I had established a steady rhythm, I reached around and pinched the boy's nips. phillippe followed suit. The boys were twisting and moaning as our cockmeat made its presence known and our vice-like grip on their nips increased.

Since this was phillippe's first time, I knew he would cum quickly and he did. Moaning, rearing his head back, he ejaculated in the boy's hole.

I ramped up my action and came a few minutes later.

The boy reared backward as the cum spurted inside his hole.

"Thank you, Sir" as he turned around and knelt before my dripping cock. I swatted the other boy and he was soon on his knees in front of phillippe's cock.

"Show your appreciation, boys," I ordered, as I pulled the boy's head toward my cock. He licked it clean. The other boy serviced phillippe's cock.

They were apparently experienced cocksuckers as they licked both our cocks expertly.

"Stand up, boy," I ordered, I kissed him hard. Once again, following my lead, phillippe grabbed his boy's head and pulling him up, tongued the boy's mouth.

"Now get down and lick your Masters' boots." There was no hesitation as the two boys got on all fours and licked my boots and my slave's boots.

"Back up," I ordered when they had finished this task.

I looked them both in the eyes and said, "We'll see you here next week for the next session."

"Yes, SIR!" they both replied, "Thank you, SIRS!"

They pulled their pants up and disappeared down the street.

We watched them as they departed.

"Good job, slave. Don't get used to it. It was a special treat."

"Yes, My Master," phillippe replied as he got down on all fours and began re-licking my boots. I patted him on the spiked hood and said, "Good boy."

THE BARTENDER IN BLACK

Maybe you don't experience this, but it happens to me all the time.

I see someone that interests me across the street or out of speaking distance and that moment of attraction is there. Whatever it might be – a boyish smile, a handsome ass, defined chest, whatever. And I'll see him again and again but never within distance to bump into him or strike up a conversation.

Well, it happened again. I had just moved to Philadelphia – accepted a job at a fairly large company. Decent salary, good benefits. It meant for me a suit and tie every working day – often on weekends. I had gotten rid of my car and purchased a motorcycle – easier to park, easier to negotiate the downtown streets, and of course, a chance to jam my ass in Leather and explore. The salary afforded me a few pleasures including a Langlitz jacket and new Dehner boots.

I had only been at the job a month or so, when I first spotted him.

Nice looking boy with an ever-present smile on his face. Liked his looks. Wondered what was underneath the worn jeans. He always wore an un-tucked shirt, so couldn't assess what kind of nips he had to pluck. Just knew that I liked his looks. The first time I saw him was on the crowded street. I was walking to work when I noticed a pair of cowboy boots walking swiftly toward me. As I looked up, there he was. Smiling. He nodded to me, but kept walking swiftly in the opposite direction. I didn't turn around even though I wanted to record his ass in my collective memory. Wouldn't have done any good – he had on one of those baggy shirts that he seemed fond of wearing. That day at work his image floated into my thoughts more than once.

Two weeks later, the same thing.

Over the next several weeks, I saw him several times – on the opposite side of the street, too far away to strike up a conversation at a street corner. He was always alone. Never in conversation with a cellphone glued to his ear.

I had been working my ass off at work for two months before I decided enough was enough. The apartment was filled with work that needed to be done before Monday, but hell, it was Friday night. I needed to be among my own kind. I stripped off the suit and tie and put on my tight black Leather pants. Studded cod, why not? Cycle jacket, gloves, Muir cap and knee-high Dehners. I was gonna check out the Leather bar that I had not been to since moving to Philly. In fact, hadn't been there for a couple of years. I wanted to slut it up, pick up a boy, take him back to my apartment and get sucked. And fuck him. The bar used to have a pretty good selection of Leather boys.

I arrived at 10:30 and the bar had a fairly thick crowd of men. Some in Leather. Most of them in tee shirts and jeans. As I entered, I seemed to be the only guy in full Leather. Oh well, wasn't the first time that had happened.

As I crossed to the bar, there he was. He was the bartender.

In a tight black tee shirt, with the name of the bar written across his chest. Nice pecs. His arms were nicely defined. I was more curious to see what was behind the bar, hidden from view. Even though I leaned forward, I couldn't see his crotch or his ass. As I ordered my beer, he nodded and smiled.

"I've seen you around town – was curious where you spent your time," I said, somewhat flirtatiously.

"Yes, Sir, I'm Tim."

"Nice to know you, Tim, I'm G.W."

"Perhaps I seem forward, but I've noticed you too, Sir."

"It's good to be noticed…" I would have continued, but two guys sidled up to the bar and ordered mixed drinks. Tim had to attend to his duties, so I found a spot along the wall. Couldn't stop watching him. Damn, I wanted him. I'll just bet he was wearing chaps and a jock. Wanted to get behind the bar and stick my spiked cod between his asscheeks. But as the midnight hour approached, Tim became busier and there were times when I couldn't even see him. I talked to several other guys but my eyes kept flickering back to him. His handsome boychest really had my attention. His smile was ever-present. Once or twice, I caught his eye and he smiled broadly.

I had almost finished my second beer, when someone tapped me on the shoulder.

It was Tim. He handed me a another beer, "Compliments of the house, Sir."

"Well, thank you, Tim," as I rested my gloved hand on his shoulder.

Damn, he was more appealing by the second. I looked down and was rewarded with a Leather jock, chaps, and the same cowboy boots I had first spotted.

I reached down and tweaked his cod. It was filled with the hard shaft and head of his boy cock.

"I'd like to continue this, Sir, but duty calls."

"Certainly, son." I swatted his ass as he returned to the bar. It was once again hidden behind the bar. My collective memory recorded those plowable asscheeks. He looked over at me several more times and smiled even more broadly.

As they were shooing people out of the bar at 2AM, I tried to catch his attention, but he was too busy and didn't look up. I hung outside the bar for a good twenty minutes, hoping he would appear, but to no avail. I had to work that Saturday anyway. Sex with a bartender would have lasted until dawn I rationalized. He was just so damned appealing – I walked with a hard-on to my apartment. I jacked off with him in mind. That thick cream running down his throat and out that smiling mouth. Looking up at me and saying, "Thank you, Daddy."

The next three weeks were brutal at work. I was working on a presentation and was at the office more than my apartment. Several nights, after hours, I changed into my Leather skins and worked on the presentation. It was relaxing and I could work more efficiently than in my suit and tie. Work Saturday. Work Sunday. My only company was a cigar when I finally got home each night.

Finally, I finished the presentation and headed out to the bar five weeks after that first night.

I sauntered into the bar and there was that cute cub. He was wearing Leather cuffs and that sexy black tee shirt. As I ordered my beer, I was not disappointed as I peeked over the bar. Leather chaps, jock, cowboy boots. I knew a handsome ass was behind it. And I wanted it in the grip of my Leather gloves.

"Hello, Sir," Tim grinned, as he handed me my beer and refused my money. "On the house, from an admirer." He smiled that generous smile. I wanted to reach over the bar and pull him toward me, thrusting my horny tongue into his throat. But, of course, patrons were already waiting behind me for their drink orders.

I thanked him, tipping the bottle toward him. I found a spot along the wall. I found myself exhibiting pangs of jealousy as I saw him interacting with other patrons. Did he flash that smile at everyone? No, it was reserved for me, I assured myself.

I just had to make contact. And what do all good Leathermen do? I borrowed a pen lying on the bar and penned a note on a cocktail napkin.

"Call me. Want to play with you..." and I wrote my name and phone number. When I went over to replenish my beer, I reached over and tucked it into the neck of his tee shirt. He smiled, but didn't immediately acknowledge it.

I spent the rest of the evening in casual conversation with several guys, but they just did not hold my interest.

I was swept out of the bar once again at closing time and waited outside for thirty minutes, but no Tim. Damn! I went home frustrated. This pick-up was not going to be easy, apparently. I fell into a fitful sleep and dreamed about the boy and me fucking.

I rushed home the next day, certain that Tim would have called. There were no phone messages. Damn. Double damn.

I checked my phone to make sure it worked. Should have given him my email, my office phone, and my fucking zip code!

This was turning into an obsession!

The next day, I was hurrying to work – I had decided to walk since it was a beautiful day and I could cover the fifteen blocks fairly rapidly.

And there he was, four blocks ahead on the other side of the street. Believe it or not, I started running to catch up to him. But by the time I reached the spot where I had seen him, he was nowhere to be seen. I was distracted the rest of the day and left early. I thought about stopping at the bar for a quick drink, but went home instead.

The next several days, I was frustrated. I wanted that boy's ass in my bed. Wanted to fuck him in Leather. Why hadn't he called?

I was on my way home from work Thursday when I once again spotted him, walking quickly. I rushed across the street and grabbed the back of his neck. He reacted violently by lashing out with a doubled-up fist. I caught it in time.

"Listen you fucking punk…," I started, right up in his face.

"Sir, please let me explain…." as his eyes welled up with tears, "I couldn't wait to read your note, but had to close the bar the night you gave it to me. As soon as I got home, I stripped off my tee shirt only to find that it was soaked in sweat and the numbers ran together… Believe me, Sir, I wanted to call you… but couldn't even read your name." He looked miserable and I instinctively knew he was telling the truth.

I loosened the grip on his neck. He sunk to his knees and clutched me around my suited legs. "I would suck your cock right here, Sir, if it would set things right."

We were in the middle of the sidewalk, with people hurrying past the scene at hand.

"No, not here, get up…" He rose and I put my arm around his shoulder.

"I want you to come to my apartment tonight, dressed in your bar uniform. Understood, boy?"

"Sir, yes, Sir," he responded as I gave him my address and told him to repeat it.

He was to arrive at 7:30, no excuses.

"Yes, Sir. Thank you, Sir, for giving me the opportunity to serve you."

"All right then, boy. Don't fuck up."

I hastened home and fixed a hasty meal. Changed into my Master Leathers, complete with my executioner's hood. Floggers attached to my belt. I rubbed my cod into fullness and lighted a big, black cigar.

Right on the dot of 7:30, a knock sounded on my door. And there he was… finally. Dressed in that black tee, his chaps and jock. A bandana covering his exposed asscheeks. And those sexy cowboy boots.

I flattened him against the wall, quickly pulling off his bar tee. My hands were all over that delicious boy. Rubbing his asscheeks, pulling on his nips, massaging his cock with my gloved hands.

"Turn around, boy." I ordered.

I flogged his ass thirty quick strokes. "That's for losing my number, boy."

His head bowed, he answered, "Yes, Sir. Thank you, Sir; I deserve it for keeping my Master waiting."

The boy took the floggings well. I pulled a full hood out of the chest of drawers in the hallway and laced his handsome face into it. His eyes looked so appealing as I turned him around once again and fondled his ass.

My cock was pulsing with an urgency of having had no sex for a long time.

As I rubbed my Leathered body against his, I pulled my cod off and massaged my already-dripping cock. Grabbing him around the middle, I repositioned him so that his ass met my cock. And with that, I inserted it into his boy hole. He twisted and turned as my manrod arched up his chute. He thanked me repeatedly as my cock made its way up his hole until my balls were slapping against his asscheeks.

I have to say, that even though it didn't last long, it was a great fuck. It didn't take me long for my cream to lubricate his ass, some cum spilling out. I gathered a gob of it, and fed it to him.

His tongue eagerly lapped it up.

My cock popped out of his hole, but I continued to molest his nips with my gloved hands.

It felt so damned good that I continued to rub my Leathers against him until I was hard once again.

Couldn't resist, stuck my pole back in with ease, as his asschute was still dripping with cum.

We played like that for a couple of hours.

Damn, was I ever horny. Just could not get enough of the boy.

Tim has become my very willing fuckboy. On call, when I need Leathersex. And I need it a lot!

And I know where my boy is every night until two. He has been instructed not to smile as generously at patrons. That smile is reserved for me. And I have ordered him to continue wearing those baggy shirts. That handsome body of the bartender in black is reserved for his Daddy's use.

TY BREAKER

My name is Gibson MacKenzie, but my friends call me Gib. I grew up in St. Louis, Missouri. My parents were down-to-earth, solid citizens and expected me to follow in their footsteps. Dad runs a heating and plumbing company, my Mom is a schoolteacher. By all accounts, I must have been a headache from the time I hit puberty. Dad wanted me to take over the family business someday, but I had other plans. I tried, I really tried. I apprenticed with Dad and worked in the company until I was twenty-six. By then, I realized I hated heating and plumbing and I wasn't going to be the marrying kind, producing grandchildren for them at regular intervals. About the time I hit puberty, I realized that I wanted to play with men. Coming out to my parents was an ordeal and I guess I was lucky they didn't just throw me out of the house. After all, I was their only child, their hope for the future…and for grandchildren. Sorry, my seed would be planted deep in the throats of willing men or in or around other male body parts.

At twenty-six, I announced that I was going to move to Tulsa, Oklahoma and open my own business – a cigar store. I had been smoking illicitly since I was about twelve. I masturbated when I saw the Marlboro man cigarette ads. Despite their disappointment, my parents still loved me as their son and wished me well in my venture, telling me that I could always come home and rejoin the family business when the cigar store failed. It made me all the more determined to succeed.

My parents had taught me to be frugal from an early age and except for necessities like beer, cigarettes and porn magazines, I had managed to sock away enough money to buy a small building in Tulsa and stock it with cigars. I had done my homework – it was the only smoke store within thirty two miles. The store also carried chew and smoking accessories. I set up a smoking lounge with comfortable Leather easy chairs in the store as well as wooden rocking chairs on the front porch.

I had been open for about two and a half weeks when the sound of a motorcycle approached the front of the store. The engine was killed, so I knew I had my first customer of the day. I looked up as a handsome man entered the store. Let me rephrase that – a Golden God had entered the store.

He was tall, well over six feet. A black Leather cowboy hat revealed a deeply tanned face, with just a few crows' feet around the sultry blue eyes. His face sported a mustache which drooped down to the chin and fanned out toward his cheeks. No chin whiskers – I guess you would call his mustache a Fu Manchu. The man wore one of those shirts – I think you call them a cavalry shirt, double-breasted with a bib front. Cornflower blue to match his eyes. Tan Leather work gloves covered his hands. Tan Leather chaps and a soft Leather pouch in which resided his cock. You could see the outline of it pressing against the tan Leather. Cowboy boots – fancy red with white tooling.

Damn, my heart was pounding. I took a long swallow before I said, "Mornin', can I help you?"

The man looked at me for a long second, "Hope so. I've been rollin' my own cigarettes for a long time – decided to try some cigars for a longer, more satisfying smoke." His eyes twinkled as his mouth opened to reveal a generous smile.

"Well, you sure came to the right place." I responded. As I exited the counter, I pulled out several cigars from the glassed-in humidor, recommending them as my personal favorites. "Why don't I put together an assortment of about ten cigars and you try them and then we'll fix you up with a bigger supply."

"That sounds fine," he remarked as he surveyed the contents of the humidor. I returned to the counter to write up the order. As he turned to look at the smoking accessories, I froze in mid writing. He had turned to reveal his asscheeks which were buck naked.

My heart started beating and my cock rose in my jeans. I started sweating.

He turned back around, catching my eyes for a moment.

"Anything wrong?" he asked, knowing full well what I had been looking at. His smile broadened as he continued to look at me.

"No, nothing." I replied, trying to appear as calmly as I could and concentrating on writing up the order.

"Don't like to get saddle sores..." he explained, as he rubbed one butt cheek with his gloved hand.

I was so tongue-tied; I didn't know how to respond, so I said nothing.

"You from around here?" he asked.

"No, I moved here from St. Louie."

"Oh, well, glad to have you here, Buddy. My name is Tyler, everybody just calls me Ty."

I introduced myself and presented him with the bill. He reached inside his chaps and extracted his wallet.

"I wondered where you carried your wallet!" I blurted out before I had a chance to think about what I was saying.

He laughed easily and so did I.

"We're pretty low key around here. I live on my parents' farm about ten miles out of town. Six hundred acres – I farm the north two hundred. When you get settled, Buddy, come on out, I'll show you around."

"I'd really enjoy that, Ty."

He paid for his purchase and tipping his hat, left the store.

I stood for a long time, my eyes freeze-framing those tanned asscheeks and the handsome man who owned them. My cock stayed hard for a long time afterward.

The business of the store picked up. There were lots of men who enjoyed a good smoke or chew. Most of them that came in wore faded jeans and you could tell from the rounded impression in their back pocket that they liked their chew. I quickly stocked the store with all their favorite brands and added a couple of copper spittoons near the seating area. I wanted them to come and linger. I stayed behind the counter a good part of the time, it disguised the hard-on I got when these men turned around and their handsome denimed asses presented themselves for my 'inspection.'

It was Wednesday when the following event occurred. Wednesday is traditionally my slowest day.

The door opened and Charlie and Bo walked in. Two of my semi-regular customers. They were both handsome, sun-weathered faces, powerful bodies packed in tight jeans and denim shirts. Usually had on their tan work gloves. Powerful asses packed into their tight Wranglers.

I greeted them and pulled each of their favorite chews off the shelf. They paid and settled themselves into two of the easy chairs.

As they settled into their mutual chairs, my eyes lingered on their muscular bodies, conditioned by years of working on their farms. Both were in their thirties – rugged, masculine, laid-back, at ease with their lives.

I was ordering inventory when I heard the familiar crank of a cycle and my heart began pumping. I knew instinctively it was Ty. I just had not had a chance to take him up on his offer to visit his farm.

His boots clicked across the floor as he acknowledged the presence of Charlie and Bo.

He was apparently used to wearing what he had on the first time I met him, because damned if he didn't have on the same chaps, with his handsome ass proudly displayed. The men didn't seem to notice, or maybe were used to it, because they said nothing, simply giving him a slap on his asscheeks with their tan, gloved hands. My cock was throbbing.

"Give me a box of these," Ty said, as he pressed into the palm of my hand the cigar ring of one of my favorite smokes.

"Sure thing, Ty" as I searched the shelves for the box.

"Then, crack it open for these fuckers. I want them to try it..."

He settled himself into one of the chairs and pulled his pack of matches from his shirt pocket.

I opened the box and presented it in turn to Ty and the two men. "Take one for yourself and join us."

I eased myself into the chair, my crotch tightened by my hard cock. That day, I had worn my tight Wranglers with a pair of chaps over them.

Ty's mouth turned up at the edges, "Looks like you left your saddle horn in your pants Gib."

I started to blush as the men hooted. They had all lighted up and were blowing smoke toward the ceiling.

The men started talking about business at their respective farms. I noticed that as they talked, each man was slowly rubbing their denimed crotches.

I was fixated on that action as Ty leaned over to me and said, "Mind if we have a little contest here?"

"Ah, no," I stuttered.

Ty's eyes sparkled as he said, "You heard the bossman".

With that, each man in turn unzipped their jeans and pulled out their lengthening rods.

I gulped as I examined each man's cock – one more impressive than the next. Ty's, of course, was the most handsome boner. Big meaty head, with a long shaft.

He absently stroked it as did the other two men, smoking and laughing at each other's comments.

"Come on, boy, pull yours out… we ain't looking."

I was reluctant at first, but hell, after all, it was my shop. With some difficulty, I pulled out my hardened bone.

It pulsed in my hand, throbbing up and down.

"Now, here's our rules…", explained Ty, "the guy who can stroke and smoke the longest…without cumming and without his cigar ash falling, is declared the winner, and gets the rest of this box."

I was the only one to nod; the other guys had already played this game several times before and were slowing down their stroking so that they could prolong their jacking off.

It was such a fucking erotic scene – these men, with their big cocks held firmly in their tan gloved hands, drawing on the cigars, blowing smoke toward the ceiling.

No one said anything. All that could be heard was the slow rubbing of a rough tan glove against a cock shaft. Sucking in on the cigars, blowing smoke out. This would have made a great porn movie.

The ash lengthened on each cigar. Slow and steady cock-rubbing. Ty's eyes were closed as I watched him. I diverted my eyes and tried not to think about this handsome man seated a few feet away from me, playing with his meat. I wanted to get down and suck him off. "No, stop it," I thought, "don't think about that man." I concentrated on slowing it down.

Ten minutes or more elapsed with not a word from any of them. I looked up to see the three faces beginning to contort as the rubbing continued.

"Ah, fuck," Charlie yelled, as a geyser of cum erupted from his healthy dick. He flicked the long ash onto his cock and sat there rubbing the ash into his man juices. Greasing his pole with the mixture.

I saw a drop of pre-cum appear out of my piss slit and willed it to stay there. "No, don't cum, not yet." My cock held firm for at least five more minutes, but I made the mistake of looking over at Ty. He was slouched down in his chair, his big, handsome cock pulsing back and forth. I shot cum down my jeans and mimicked Charlie's action, by flicking my ash and mixing it in with the cum. "Damn, never thought about doing that," as I rubbed it all over my cock. "I'm out," I declared simply. Only Charlie seemed to notice. He gave me a knowing wink.

The contest was now between Ty and Bo. Bo had his eyes closed and was doing a lazed rubbing of his meat. His ash was a good three inches long. It looked as if it would drop at any minute.

Ty was still slouched in his chair, his booted foot crossed over the other. He took long drags on his cigar with an easy air of confidence expressed by the satisfied smile on his face.

Charlie and I watched the two remaining contestants as the minutes ticked by.

Both ashes were at least four inches long. Both cocks were fully tumescent. Damn, I wanted to suck them both off.

Just then, Bo's ash dropped, spilling all over the front of his pants. His cock seemed to reach upward, attempting to catch some of the ash in his piss slit and with that it 'blew'. A load of cum coursed out of his cock and he simply muttered 'Shit'.

"You win, you fucker," he announced to Ty. It was only then that Ty opened his eyes and crowed, "I knew I would. I've been practicing for a couple of weeks!" He chortled at his own remark as he stroked his cock to a satisfying ejaculation.

With that, the men eased back into their conversation and I exited to the counter.

The contest became a regular feature at the cigar store, usually after hours. More men joined the group. Seemed that Ty always won.

A good month and a half had elapsed and I had a regular clientele.

Each time Ty came in, he invited me to view the workings of his farm.

Finally, on a Saturday afternoon, I closed the store thirty minutes early, determined to visit the handsome man in his own surroundings.

I made sure I had my tightest, most faded jeans on, along with a denim work shirt and my brand new black cowboy boots.

I got in my truck and drove the short distance to Ty's ranch – the Circle J ranch.

I drove through the gates and down the long, dirt lane. Rounding a bend in the lane, I viewed a small farmhouse. Knew it was Ty's. His cycle was parked out front, gleaming in the sun. Ty was leaning against a post, a cigar clenched between his teeth. He was shirtless, nice looking nips planted firmly in the middle of his sexy, washboard stomach. He wore the familiar golden chaps and tan pouch.

A smile developed as I stepped out of my truck.

I approached him, raising my hand in greeting. He grabbed me and thrust his tongue down my throat. We kissed long and hard as I felt his strong hand squeeze my left ass cheek.

"About time you got here," Ty said, as he released me and slapped my ass cheek for good measure. "Come on in." He even held the door for me.

The house was comfortably furnished with Leather easy chairs and a big portrait of Ty over the fireplace. It was a virtual duplicate of what he was wearing. Same chaps, same pouch. His fucking hard dick outlined in the pouch. There was no mistaking the big meaty head and the shaft in the portrait. His gloved hands tucked into the chaps. Those handsome nips erect. That handsome bushy mustache.

"Hell, you can tell I like myself, can't you?" he said, as he retrieved two beers from the refrigerator in the nearby kitchen, "Had it painted a year or so ago… not that I'm vain or anything."

I recovered my ability of speech to say, "You have every right to be."

He strode over to me, facing me. Holding the beers in one hand, clenching the cigar between his teeth, he hooked his thumb into my jeans waistband. He pulled me closer. Removing the cigar, he pulled my jaw toward his and we engaged in a longer exploration of each other's mouths. I could feel my heart thumping and my cock pressing against my jeans.

When we finally released each other's tongues, he pulled away. Gave me a long, once-over look. "Make yourself comfortable," as he presented me with my beer. I took a long swig and as I was doing so, his gloved hand began unbuttoning my shirt.

I shivered; I wanted to feel that sun-burned body against mine. The shirt was discarded on the floor as he pressed his handsome chest against my own excited nips. His gloved hands reached around and cupped my asscheeks. I could feel his hard bone in that tan pouch pressed against my own hardened cock.

His right hand reached around and started to unzip my jeans. They fell around my knees. His rough Leather glove began pulling on my cock, alternately stroking my balls.

He reached down and pulled out his own cock, throbbing. Heavily veined. He grabbed both cocks and began stroking the two together. I was breathing heavily, trying to control my cum. I closed my eyes, feeling that not-so-gentle stroking of our two cocks. I briefly opened my eyes, only to view Ty's head rearing back. He too was breathing heavily.

His grip increased, pressing down on my cock shaft. Feeling his bone against mine. I could now feel his breath, interspersed with bursts of smoke from his cigar.

I could feel the cum rise in my cock, my cock pulsing, begging for release. The grip only increased, now pressing against the base of the cock.

I could feel his cock's head pressing into the area between my cock and balls.

I heard him utter the words, "Circle J" as his cock released his man juices. I could no longer control my cum and released my cum at the same time. Both our cocks were slathered in mancum. We both stood breathing heavily until I felt him scoop up a load of cum and a rough glove was soon forced into my mouth. I ate it greedily. He filled my mouth three times with gobs of creamy cum, assumedly collected from both our cocks.

He pulled my head toward his, and once again, we kissed for a very long time.

Finally, the session ended. He pulled away to take a long swig of beer and relight his cigar which had gone out. I stood uncertainly for a few minutes, but finally pulled my jeans up around my waist, but didn't zip them. His cock was hanging out of his pouch, still dripping remnants of cum.

"Damn, that felt good, son," Ty finally said, as he stood near the fireplace, one hand resting on the rough-hewn wooden beam which served as a mantle.

He turned toward the mantle and spread his arms across the wide mantelpiece, his hole raised.

"Fuck me," he said simply.

I gulped. Swallowed hard. I approached him as he twisted his ass left and right. He turned his head, saying, "Fuck me. I want your cock in my hole."

I had always thought of myself as submissive to other men.

I don't know what came over me – maybe it was the release after not having sex since I had moved, but my horniness took over.

"Damn right," I said as I approached him and pushed him roughly against the mantelpiece. He didn't object as I started pulling on his nips. I took the opportunity to press my body against his, squeezing his asscheeks. My cock hardened and so was his. Despite the fact that we had just shot, our cocks were hardened again. I soon lubed my cock and entered his manhole. Like I said, I hadn't had sex since I had moved to Tulsa and sure as hell was gonna make up for lost time. Within a period of time, not sure how long it was, my cock pumped jism up his hole. He moaned and his cum came shooting out, splattering on the firewood in the fireplace below. He turned and our cum combined as I held our cocks firmly in my right hand. Cum shooting all over each other's cocks. Our mouths hungrily eating each other's cream.

I pushed him roughly on the floor and crawled on top of him. He did not resist. My hungry mouth covered his. We grabbed and tugged at each other. I spit in his face and rubbed the saliva on my gloved hand. I pressed my gloved hand into his mouth and he sucked on it. I slapped him on the left cheek and then the right. I reached down and fondled his hardening cock.

"Please, Sir, I need your cock in my hole again," he begged.

I straddled him as I rolled him over on the floor. His beautiful asscheeks were inviting my dick to explore. My dick hardened quickly as I spit on it for lubrication and then eased it up his manhole. He moaned as it inched further into that beautiful fuck-hole. He spread his arms on the floor as I began to pump slowly, but aggressively. His moaning continued as my dick enlarged inside him. I was beginning to breathe heavily as my cock gathered its man juices for a third time that afternoon. I began thrusting more violently as I reared up and placed my hands on his ribcage.

We were both sweating as the exertion of mansex increased in intensity.

He was moaning steadily, my heart was pounding as my cock's juices rose to the head and with a final thrust; I poured my mancum into that ass outlined in those handsome tan chaps.

As I shot my load, his ass cheeks clenched shut, holding my cock prisoner until the last drop of cum was squeezed out. We both were immobilized by the fucking that had just taken place.

We spent the rest of the afternoon fucking and sucking.

Since that afternoon, I visit the Circle J quite frequently and Ty has become my best customer – in more ways than just the sale of tobacco. If I could bottle the mancum that has erupted from both our cocks, I'd be a fucking millionaire. Nope, not planning on returning to heating and plumbing any time soon. Got Ty's plumbing to explore and already have enough heat for an inferno.

UP AGAINST IT

Jerry liked rough sex. He craved it. He had grown up tough. His old man, a biker, had slapped him around quite a bit as a kid. When he was sixteen, Jerry had grabbed his old man's Leathers and wallet while his old man was sleeping off a drunken stupor, took the keys to his old man's Harley and set out on his own. He had never looked back.

Fifteen years later, Jerry had landed in Pittsburgh. Earning enough during the day to keep himself in rent and food and free enough to cruise the alleys of Pittsburgh. He usually ended up roughing up his play partners in what were a series of one-night stands. He had given up on the bars – just a bunch of fucking twinks.

Tonight was different. Jerry had recently acquired a computer and spent the days cruising for sites which would satisfy his desires. He finally found a site devoted to big men. Rough fuckers – tattoos, bikes, head-to-toe Leather, rough sex preferred. He wanted to experience being taken.

Have his hole stretched. See how it felt. He knew he could take it.

He had connected with a man named SSBruder. He guaranteed the reader that he was 100% top, no mercy shown as he plowed the ass of his recipient. Jerry looked at the pics and his dick hardened. This guy had no soul – his black eyes peered out at the reader.

Jerry arranged to meet the dude at 1:30 am in an alley near the north side of town. Jerry idled his cycle down and hid it discretely behind a building. He marched toward the alley. The streets were deserted. Perfect.

The alley was unlighted. Dark as shit. Jerry's boots clicked on the pavement as he found a length of brick wall. It was marked with graffiti which read, "Ass fucking in progress." That was the sign under which he was to rendezvous.

Jerry lighted a cigar and propped his left foot against the wall. His father's Leather chaps hugged his denimed ass – 'one thing my old man gave me – a nice ass' His old Leather jacket zipped to the mid-chest, holding his nipclamps in place. He never wore a shirt – he liked the feeling of raw Leather against his tits. Jerry was excited about the impending session as he continued to drag on the cigar. His other hand fondled his hardened cock through his worn 501s. In the distance, the traffic on the expressway whizzed past, seemingly speeding up to get through the dangerous portion of the city.

Jerry reached into his jacket and extracted a flask, taking a swig of pure whiskey. It tasted good in combination with the tobacco. The traffic lulled him into thinking about his old man. He repositioned himself, leaning on his left shoulder against the brick wall.

Without warning, a gloved hand clamped over his mouth. The other hand quickly wrenched Jerry's left wrist in back of him. A handcuff was clicked into place. Before Jerry could resist, the handcuffs clamped around his right wrist. His Muir cap was knocked off and a black Leather hood was inserted over his face. Jerry caught only a momentary glimpse of the big Leatherman, with an executioner's hood in place before the hood was being laced over his own head. No eyeholes, just a mouth hole. His cigar, which had been in his right hand, was now jammed into his mouth. His body was wrenched toward the brick wall and slammed against it. He could feel the strength of the big man as he surrounded Jerry. His cod pressed into Jerry's asscheeks, separated only by the worn denim of his 501s. The man's big chest flattened against Jerry's back. Jerry was breathing heavily, but his cock was fully aroused.

The man began thrusting his codpiece against Jerry's ass. He held Jerry's arms painfully in back of him. Jerry could smell the big man's cigar.

The big man was talking, but it was in low, whispered tones. Jerry's ears strained to hear what the man was saying.

The Leatherman reached around and slowly unzipped Jerry's jacket. Jerry's nipclamps were now pressed painfully against the wall, but the pain was nothing like that now exerted on his nips as the Leatherman twisted the clamps to the left and then to the right. Titclamps biting into his man-tits. After a time, the Leatherman's hands reached down and unsnapped Jerry's chaps and then unbuttoned the 501s. His big meaty, glove-covered hand squeezed Jerry's cock and balls. The pain was delicious as Jerry's head arched backward.

The Leatherman's gloved hands smoothed around Jerry's hips pulling Jerry's pants down and revealing his ass. Jerry's ass flexed as the Leatherman swatted the asscheeks and then began exploring Jerry's hole with the softness of his black Leather gloved hands. The big studded cod soon was pressing against it. The Leatherman continued to press his Leathered body against Jerry's ass as the Leatherman ripped his cod off his pants. His big bullcock was soon out, taking the evening air, but seeking an appropriate hole to burrow in.

It didn't take him long to thrust that big fucking man meat up Jerry's hole and despite Jerry's toughness. He moaned as the cock's head and shaft made its way up Jerry's fuck-hole.

His ass began throbbing. His hole constricting, trying to force out the invader man spade, but to no avail. The Leatherman clamped his arms around Jerry's midsection and began pumping.

The man's hooded head leaned toward his fuck toy, "Feels good, huh, fuckboy?" as his cock inched up the boy's abused hole.

The Leatherman reached up and twisted the nipclamps, which added further pain to Jerry's tortured nips.

Despite any pain he felt, Jerry was enjoying it. He loved the roughness, the rawness of the encounter. Now, he knew what it felt like. He enjoyed it. He could take it. His ass began to relax and seemingly absorbed the man's cock into his hole. His head was resting against the brick wall.

His abused tits were throbbing. His hole was being violated and he wanted more. He wanted to grab the man's meat and push it in harder.

He wanted the man's Leathered body to slam against him repeatedly. He wanted that dick to shoot cream so that it came out his mouth.

The man was thrusting harder and harder and with a mighty body slam, his cum-juices released up Jerry's hole.

Swiftly, Jerry was turned around and pushed to his knees. Without ceremony, the man thrust his big bulldick in Jerry's mouth and Jerry gratefully licked the cream off the Leatherman's cock. He licked it until it was clean.

The Leatherman unlaced the captured victim's hood, opened the handcuffs and reinserting them on his belt, slapped Jerry's face several times and disappeared into the night.

Jerry remained on his knees, exhausted. His ass and nips aching.

As he began to stand up, a big Leatherman strode toward Jerry.

"Get up, you asshole, face against the wall." As he looked toward the hooded man's eyes, he realized that this was the guy with which he had an appointment. "Who the fuck was the other guy?" Jerry momentarily thought, as his body was slammed against the wall and the ass fucking began in earnest.

BOOTLICKER ED

Dedicated to my bootlicking Leatherbuddy Ed

It was the eve of my birthday and in anticipation of the event, I was looking on the internet for a birthday gift for myself. Hell, why not? I deserved it. I knew it would be Leather – just didn't know what it would be until I saw it. Looked at chaps, pants, jackets, boots. You have to understand I have a large collection of Leather gear – after all, I'm a confirmed Leatherman and wear my Leathers every day. But I wanted something different. Something I didn't have.

And I was looking at used gear. I didn't say I was rich. And I like the idea of wearing another man's worn Leathers.

As I was cruising through boots, there they were. A pair of cowboy boots. The damned red tooling on them caught my eye. I flag 'red' to the left and thought these would be a good compliment to the red hanky in my back pocket. Eighteen inches. And those damned toes were so fucking pointy – could just envision them separating a handsome boy's asscheeks. And as a bonus, they came with silver spurs. Instead of bidding on them, I clicked 'Buy Now' and made a PayPal payment before any other Leather guy could snap them up. According to the description, they were worn by a bona fide cowboy in Nevada. Fuck, HOT! Wish a picture of him was part of the deal, but my imagination would just have to suffice. They were beyond my budget, but my Leather soul told me I had to have them.

Now, the waiting game. They were being shipped from Nevada – 5 to 7 business days. Fuck.

Each day, I waited anxiously to hear the familiar brown truck which delivered such goods. One day I was waiting on my porch and the truck just sailed by. Next day and the day after that, same thing happened.

The next day I had been out on errands and anxiously eyed the back porch for a large package – nothing. Shit.

On the seventh day, God rested. Or so, says the Bible. But this Leatherman wasn't resting. I was pacing on the porch floor. Full Leather – my comfortable old Harley boots on. Smoking a stogie after lunch.

And then it happened. I heard the familiar brown truck entering my driveway. Couldn't quite see what the driver was extracting from the back, but I anticipated him carrying that large package and presenting it to me as if I was a kid on Christmas morning.

What I didn't expect was that the driver was a handsome man. He wore the familiar brown shorts and a tight brown shirt. And, unexpectedly, he had on a pair of Wescos to the knee, tightly laced.

At this point, I was more interested in the package below his waist. Damn, he was devilishly handsome.

"Good afternoon, Sir" he greeted me, with an easy smile.

"Afternoon, hope you brought me my birthday present."

"Well, Sir, it's addressed to you if you're G.W."

"That's me," as he climbed the steps to the porch.

"Sign here, Sir," as he handed me the pad. I quickly scrawled my name and said, "I've been anxiously awaiting these."

"Oh, Sir?"

"Yeah, a pair of boots to add to my collection." A bead of sweat appeared on his forehead as the delivery boy continued to eye the package. I noticed too that he had taken in my Leather pants with the attached spiked cod.

He licked his lips, appearing almost speechless. "Uh, Sir... mind if I see them?"

I pulled the knife off my belt and slit the box open. They were carefully wrapped in bubble wrap, but soon the handsome boots came into view. The boy craned his neck to view them.

I noticed the boy was sweating as I held them up for him to view.

They were... beautiful. No other word can describe them. The hand-tooling done in red. Those fucking nasty spurs. I held out one boot and the boy clutched it to his face. He began licking the toe.

"Sir," he stammered, "allow me to put them on your feet... please?"

"Well, sure, son," I answered as I sat down in my chair.

He reverently removed my old Harleys and placed them to the side. Left boot. I lifted my foot. He held the boot against his chest and began easing it on my foot. He was breathing heavily and nuzzled the toe with his cheek. Same with the right boot.

His eyes were fixed on the boots and I had a feeling I knew what was coming.

He bowed his head and whispered, "Sir, may I be privileged to lick your boots?"

I lifted his head, "Tell me your name."

"ed, Sir."

"You have my permission, bootboy ed. However, shirt off."

He rose and quickly stripped his shirt off. Nice handsome chest. Trim. Nice nips. My gloved hands reached out and began squeezing his nips.

The boy began moaning. I then pushed his head down on the right boot and he began a tongue massage. His tongue flicked in and out. His mouth was engulfed on the pointed toes and the undercut heels. Tracing the red tracery up to the tops of the boot.

Damn, I was getting a hard-on from the massage. He licked the boot over and over until I pulled my foot away and made him lick the other boot. He flicked the spur with his tongue. As he knelt lower and lower, I pressed the spur of the boot not being serviced into his back. The wheel of the spur made a pattern on his back, but he didn't even seem to notice. He just kept tonguing the boot, his eyes closed. Moaning softly.

I massaged my cod until my rod was fully extended and requesting escape from its Leather enclosure.

His hands were now massaging my calves, but I could see his eyes watching the cod grow.

"Sir, permission to lick your cod."

Yep, I wanted that tongue massage on my cod and what it held. His head rested in my lap as his tongue flicked in between the spikes on the cod. I could feel his tongue tracing the outline of my cockshaft.

Without ceremony, I reached down and ripped off the cod, releasing my mancock.

He needed no instruction as his mouth went down on my rod. Tonguing it vigorously, momentarily letting it escape his mouth to lick my balls.

I lost track of time, but I was ready to shoot sooner than later. I pushed his head back down on my cock and exploded in his mouth.

Briefly catching his eyes, he looked like he had reached nirvana. This far off look in his eyes proved to me that he was in sub heaven.

Recovering, he simply said, "Sir, permission to shoot."

"No, not yet."

I repositioned him on the porch floor after unbuckling his pants. I pulled them down around his knees and stuck the pointed toe between his asscheeks. He was squirming, moaning, begging. "Please, Sir, please, let me shoot."

"No!" as I stuck the pointed toe further up his ass.

"Sir, please," he begged once again.

"Permission denied, boy." as I continued to wiggle the toe back and forth in his boy hole.

At this point, he was gritting his teeth and grimacing.

"Roll over, boy."

The boy did and his cock was fully extended. I ground the boot into the top of his cock and then playfully lifted his cock with the toe of the boot. I knew what effect it would have as he shot a load all over my new boot. Cords of cum from his cock fully lathered the toe of the boot.

"Now, lick it off, boy," as I smiled down at the sweaty boy.

"YES, SIR! My pleasure, SIR!"

He licked every drop. His hair hung down across his sweaty forehead. He was breathing heavily.

"SIR, THANK YOU, SIR!"

"Come back tomorrow. I want you to lick them again."

The boy complied. Day after day. The same scene. Only I was the one making a number of deliveries… to his ass and throat.

RAPE ON THE BALCONY

It started out as a prank. Barry and I had been friends for about three years. We had met at a Leather bar. And with the way things were disintegrating in the Leather bar scene, he and I were the only Leather guys at the bar on their Leather and Levi night. I should amend that – we were the only men in full Leather. Some of the guys had vests on. Some had their jeans tucked into knee high boots, but he and I were the only ones in full Leather – both dressed as uniform cops. Shiny boots, Sam Browne belts. Gun belts without the guns.

We struck up an easy conversation and chugged a couple of beers before realizing that the pickings were mighty slim. We left together and spent the night playing. Really little chemistry between us – we simply went through the motions of talking dirty to one another and jacking off. He just wasn't my type. I'm a top and I like my boys to have a boyish quality. Whether it is a bubble ass or a boyish smile or a slender waist to grab and pull toward me. Barry was big and beefy. Guess he kind of looks like me. He was more attracted to me than I to him.

Anyway. We continued to rendezvous at the bar and occasionally went out to dinner. During the course of the next three years, we talked about our hopes, our dreams, and in his case, his fantasies. He had a helluva lot of 'em! Well, so did I, but unfortunately, they just didn't involve Barry.

On the night in question, Barry was approaching his fortieth birthday. A week or so before, I had taken him out to dinner at a little restaurant that catered to men who were attracted to other men. We wore our cop uniforms. The restaurant even permitted cigar smoking before dinner in a cigar lounge.

As we stoked our cigars and downed our drinks, Barry leaned forward and said, "Benton, I have got to tell you, I had a great dream last night..."

I rolled my eyes, "Another one, Barry? You must keep a journal – it must cover volumes."

"But, listen..." as he leaned forward, "this one was so real, I creamed..."

"Barry, you always cream after a wet dream, that's nothing new..."

"No, this one was different, I felt like it was really happening..."

As I settled in with a refreshed drink from the handsome waiter, I said, "Okay, tell me about it."

"I was at this black tie party... all these women in low-cut gowns and all the guys in tuxes, and so was I... This guy arrived and caught the attention of everyone in the room... he was in a fucking Leather tuxedo. Black hair, rim beard, stubble on his cheeks. Damn, was he handsome! I could feel my cock rise in my pants."

"Uhm hmm," I replied as I drew on my cigar, "what next?"

"Well, this guy came into the center of the room. Everybody was looking at him."

I was trying to stay interested, but was watching the ass of that cute little waiter as he collected orders from the smokers in the lounge.

"He looked around the room several times. And I was trying to catch his eye."

"And he found you irresistible?" I interjected.

"After four or five sweeps of his eyes, his eyes settled on me. I smiled at him and nodded. He nodded and smiled back."

"Our table should be ready soon...," I started to say, as he interrupted.

"No, listen, then... he pulled out a pair of handcuffs and wrenching my wrists behind my back, he locked them into place."

That caught my interest. "Okay, and then what?"

"He escorted me to a corner of the room, walking closely behind me. I don't think anyone really noticed that he slipped these cuffs on me. His moment in the spotlight was over and everyone resumed what they were doing. He got me to the corner..."

"Sirs, your table is ready...," the cute waiter announced and stood until we had stubbed out our cigars, picked up our drinks, and followed him to the table.

Over dinner, Barry recounted the rest of the dream.

When I returned home, I began to formulate a plan. Barry had revealed to me that he was attending a function the following Saturday. What if I made his fantasy come true?

Just by chance, I do have a Leather tuxedo. Bought it when my partner Michael and I went to the opera. God, how I hated those damned occasions. Ugly, fat women bellowing out unintelligible lyrics. Usually the male performers were attractive, though – bears with big white beards. I did it for Michael. He was passionate about opera. I feigned interest because I knew after the opera we would go home and fuck until dawn. That's how keyed up Michael would become.

I polished my knee high boots until they shone. Tucked my gloves in the jacket pocket, along with several other necessities.

The party started at 7. I arrived at 8:15, fashionably late and swept in as if invited. No one paid any particular attention to me as I circulated through the crowd. Most men were in tuxes – the Leather tuxedo blended in. If they had looked closely though, they would have noticed my codpiece. Black studs in a patterning of snakeskin. Even though I circulated through the crowd with drink in hand, I just could not spot Barry.

Finally, I spotted him. He was standing off to the left, in conversation with an older man.

I approached them, "Barry, old friend, how are you?" as I reached to shake his hand.

There was a look of surprise on Barry's face as he acknowledged my presence. His surprise though got the better of him and he said, "What are you doing here?"

"Why, I came to enjoy this evening, just like you…"

He introduced me to the man, who excused himself after a few moments of conversation.

"Damn, Benton, I was working on him to come home with me."

"Sorry, we have other plans," as I stepped behind him and quietly extracted the black handcuffs in my pocket.

"Huh, what do you mean?" Barry replied, as I pulled his right wrist behind him and snapped the handcuff in place.

"Just giving you an added bonus for your birthday," I said, as I quickly snapped his left wrist into place.

"Are you kidding, Benton? Here?"

"Walk slowly toward the east balcony, Barry," as I placed my left hand on the small of his back and pushed him gently.

A bead of sweat appeared on his forehead as he slowly maneuvered through the crowd.

Once out on the balcony, I quickly realigned the cuffs so they were encircling one of the columns supporting the balcony. I closed the French doors that led to the balcony.

"Benton, what the hell are you doing?"

"I told you... enjoying the evening." I pulled out my carefully folded Executioner's hood and laced it over my face. I pulled on my tight black Leather gloves as he whispered, "Are you fucking crazy?"

"Just fulfilling your fantasy..." I answered, as I unzipped his tuxedo pants and pulled out his big meaty cock. I began to massage it with my gloved hands and despite his protests, his cock stiffened.

My cock was aroused as well. I rubbed it in its cod with my free hand.

Letting go of it momentarily, I pulled out my cigar case and clipped two cigars; I lighted them and jammed one in his mouth. "Just two men enjoying the evening air," as I unbuttoned the top of his pants. They slid down his legs, revealing his meaty ass.

I just couldn't resist, I began slapping it with my gloved hands.

The party was in full swing, dance music had started, and no one was paying a God's bit of attention to the molesting that was transpiring on the east balcony.

I rested my cod against his asscheeks. Barry was still not into the scene, but he soon would be if I had my way with him.

My cock was pressing for release as I unsnapped the cod and let my manrod slap against his naked asscheeks.

"Benton, are you sure no one is watching?" I peered through the French doors. "Nope, no one is watching me fuck you" as I spit on my cock and slid it up his hole.

He began moaning, leaning over, taking my manrod up his hole.

I grabbed him around the hips and began a thrusting, easing in and out.

I have to say that Barry was taking it just fine. He was really getting into the scene. We could hear the music building in intensity. The music was eclectic that evening. As

I peered through the windows, the crowd was enraptured by Mendelssohn's 'Hebrides Overture', with lots of loud crashing, building up, symbolizing waves crashing.

I pounded my meat into his cave.

Barry began gasping, "Benton, oh, my God! Benton, fuck me... fuck me hard."

And of course, the birthday boy got his wish.

My cock felt like a fucking ramrod being jammed into the hole of a cannon. I fucked him harder and harder. My cock was so hard, I wasn't sure that I could release my cum. But, I did. Oh, yeah. Oh, fucking yeah. If the party had released fireworks, this would have been the time to do it.

Barry emitted a scream, but the music assumedly drowned it out. No one came running to witness the rape on the balcony.

Soon, Barry whispered, "Sir, please jack me off. My cock is aching..."

I reached around and all I had to do was to touch his pulsing cock and it exploded. It splattered all over the trunk of the potted palm nearby.

And just that quickly, I removed the handcuffs, tucked them in my pocket, and exited through the French doors. My executioner's hood in place.

I apparently made quite an appearance as I exited, hearing several people say, "Who was that masked man?"

Well, I ain't the fucking Lone Ranger.

GARDENING WITH MY BOY

If I do one thing well, it's sweating.

Maybe because I sit most of the day at a computer in my white-collar job, I crave physical activity. And my yard certainly lends itself to good, sweaty physical activity. And the damned yard seems to be the perfect breeding ground for every fucking weed known to mankind.

It was a Saturday, with nothing planned. Until Kyle called. "Daddy, Sir, I'd like to come over for a session this afternoon, Sir. If you are not already engaged with another boy. Please, Sir, your boy craves it."

I assured him that I would make time for him. He was a handsome, beefy boy. With a nice chest, muscular arms, and the most handsome ass. I instructed him to wear chaps, boots, his Leather rebel hat, and a jock. Anything else would be removed.

After eating a late breakfast, I headed out with my work gloves, clippers, and a cigar tucked in my mouth. Leather cod pants, my old shitkicker boots, a vest, and my Muir cap. We had gotten a fair amount of rain and the weeds had popped up every place. I started the assault and pretty soon, despite a nice cooling breeze, I had broken into a pretty healthy sweat. I enjoyed the scent of sun-warmed Leather and my mansweat combined. My pits were quick in producing that ripe, salty smell that I particularly enjoyed. I assumed my crotch was producing the same scent. I worked on, quickly forgetting the rest of the world. Alternate pulling, clipping, puffing on my cigar, and wiping sweat from my forehead with my red bandana. The red bandana which normally resides in my left back pocket was soon saturated with my sweat.

I certainly lost track of time even though as I would survey the property, it looked as if I had made very little progress.

Hoped I was giving the nosy neighbors quite a show as I turned my sweaty body away from them and stretched my ass in their direction. They quickly retreated to their house, but I could feel their eyes watching me as I stretched and pulled weeds left and right.

Of course, I took frequent breaks to squeeze my nips or to fondle my cod.

I was saturated with good man sweat, the back of my pants and vest clung to my body. Damn, it felt good as the breeze would kick up and I would be encouraged to do a little more.

I had been at it for two hours or more when I heard a cycle drive down my graveled driveway. It was my boy Kyle. Looking as handsome and beefy as I had ever seen him.

My cock rose as he approached me and knelt in front of me. He rubbed his left cheek against my extended cod, but I pushed his head away. Time for that a little later.

I retrieved a pair of work gloves for my boy and instructed him to remove his tee shirt. It was carelessly tossed over a fence picket. I roughly squeezed his nips and he moaned. His mouth flew open and I brought his head toward mine, giving him a hard kiss and tonguing.

"A little later for that, son, I want you to work up a healthy sweat just like your Dad."

"Yes, Sir," he replied and we returned to where I had momentarily stopped. As he was a city boy, I had to instruct him as to what to pull, what to be careful in pulling (like poison ivy which had started to make its appearance) and what were my plantings. He enjoyed taking orders and was a quick learner. With his help, we quickly accomplished the rest of the back gardens. He was sweating, the beads of sweat dripping down from his chin onto his handsome pecs. Beads of sweat on the fine, blonde fur that covered those pecs. The boy was irresistible, but as a Leather Dad, I had to exhibit some self-control. It wasn't easy. Several times when I looked over, his naked ass was stretched in my direction, his legs planted far apart. That boy hole was so fucking inviting. I controlled my man urges and went back to the business of weeding – clearing them away from my row of spindly pine trees which would ultimately give me absolute privacy from the neighbors.

One area of privacy, however, is an old stone wall, the remains of a stone house which had been refashioned into a four foot wall by one of the previous owners. It provided a nice shield from the outside world and the perfect place to take a boy for discipline and some ass fucking. We just needed to clear away the tall weeds that stood in front of it.

"Boy, come over here," I ordered as I wiped the sweat from my brow, "Let's clear this area next."

"Yes, Sir," he replied as he hastened over to me. He bent over and began pulling the weeds out by the roots. One plant seemed to have a deep taproot and as he was pulling, it resisted. Losing his balance, he tumbled against the wall. It was too much. My cock acted like a divining rod. Before he could retrieve his balance, I was straddling his ass and rubbing my cod against his asscheeks. "Oh, Dad...," the boy began moaning as the Leather rubbed against his moist ass.

My hands clamped around his waist, as I commanded for him to stay in position. He didn't argue – I didn't think he would.

I reached down and unsnapped my cod and my hungry cock sprang forth. The sweat of his body acted as a natural lubricant as I eased my male fuckrod up his hole.

I leaned my sweaty body on his broad back, massaging his muscular arms and reaching around and tweaking his sweaty nips. The work gloves worked his nips as his head arched upward. He was moaning and thanking me as my cock arched up his fuck-hole. It seemed to enlarge exponentially as it inched up his hole.

The sweat poured off of me, dripping onto his back. I wiped it off and let him taste the saltiness from the fingers of my gloves.

I wish I could say the scene lasted for hours, but my cock was hornier than normal and I soon shot a clot of cum up his ass. His ass muscles trapped my cock inside his hole, squeezing the last of the cum from my cockhead. I nuzzled his neck, kissing his cheeks.

I didn't want to take my cock out – it felt great. It didn't seem to be shrinking... From my vest pocket, I extracted a cigar and lighted it. I puffed on it contentedly as I slid my manrod back and forth in the warm cave it found refuge. I withdrew it, only to insert my gloved fist up his stretched hole. The bulky work glove would only go so far, but my boy was twisting and squirming as the raw Leather penetrated his hole. I was hard once again and for a second time, I fucked him. The cum spurted out of his hole as I pulled my cock out. I turned the boy over and lay on top of him. His back arched against the stone wall. His muscular arms gripped my waist for support. We kissed long and hard. Sweat dripping from my forehead and chest on to the boy's handsome, sweaty body.

I blew smoke in his face as he begged me to feed him forced smoke. Now what Dad could resist such a simple request? He took my smoke well. Our cocks pressed against one another's. Our nips pressed against one another's. Kissing. Giving my smoke. Fondling him. Squeezing his asscheeks. Pulling on his nips. Pulling his balls.

Damn, what a great scene.

"Let's adjourn to the dungeon, boy."

I led him into the dungeon where he quickly climbed onto the bondage table. I lay on top of him and we began an extended session.

The weeds began growing. The hell with the weeds – I was more interested in a taproot between my legs that was growing hard and firm.

Crawling off of him, I pulled him forward, under his shoulders, until his head hung below the level of the bench.

I stood on a concrete block to give me the necessary height and eased my horny taproot into his mouth. He tongued the underside of my shaft and licked the head of my cock. I began pulling it in and out, his tongue moistening every inch of it. My balls tickled his nose and I eased them into his mouth. His hands reached up and massaged my Leathered thighs. Thrusting my cock in and out that was covered in boy spit. His tongue flickered in and around my cock shaft. I reached down and pulled on his nips. That seemed to trigger a more urgent response as I knew it would.

My cock was hard and throbbing and I could feel it pressing against the roof of his mouth. His lips closed down on the base of the shaft and my cock was now fully in his mouth. Didn't take me long to shoot another load. He sucked my bone until I had no more jism to offer. He continued sucking for a long time. What a boy. An expert at extracting the natural juices from a man's taproot.

MASTER OF CEREMONIES

Every year, Drew hosted a Leather party on the anniversary of his first conquest as a Leatherman. It had been the night that he suited up and headed to the Eagle for an evening of socializing and his emergence as a top. He had paid his dues, serving as a boy to a rough Master. His Master had taught him a lot and then, when the Master felt that Drew had learned all that he could teach him, he declared his boy a Master of Leather and presented him with a Muir cap. The final accessory in his Leather wardrobe. Through his Master, Drew had earned his jock, boots, harness, gloves, chaps and finally a Leather jacket.

Drew marched proudly to the bar in full Leather gear, his Muir cap placed squarely on his head. He hesitated after retrieving his beer, only momentarily, until he spotted a suitable candidate. He strode confidently over to the boy and motioned with his gloved hand for the boy to follow him outside to the bar patio.

"On your knees, boy."

The boy obeyed him without question, never making eye contact. Drew rested his booted foot on the boy's upper thigh.

"Lick your Master's boot, boy."

The boy tentatively licked the top of the man's boot and looked up questioningly.

"I'll tell you when to stop, boy."

The boy licked the boot more vigorously and soon found the remaining boot raised for licking.

Drew swatted the boy's head a couple of times until the boy had finished his boot worshipping.

"Up, boy."

"Yes, Sir," the boy replied and stood, his head still lowered.

"What is your desire, boy?"

"To serve a Leather Master, Sir."

"Good answer," Drew replied, "Follow me."

Drew led the willing boy to his car. He retrieved wrist restraints, a recent purchase, and quickly buckled them into place around the boy's wrists, padlocking them in front of the boy.

He motioned for the boy to crawl into the passenger seat, and after buckling the seat belt, hopped into the driver's seat and sped away.

His first capture of a Leather boy was now complete and the rest is history, as they say. After six months of intense training, Drew accepted lawson as his slave.

Over the several years since that event, Drew had developed quite a roster of Leathermen as friends. Living in San Francisco was Drew's dream – the Leathermen and men into kinky sex play were abundant. And Drew was an easygoing fucker, easy on the eyes too. He enjoyed the company of his fellow Leathermen. And since play at the bars was virtually non-existent and the Leather bar were increasingly filled with twinks and the curious, Drew preferred to host his own parties, complete with cigars, liquor, and plenty of handsome young men to fuck.

Each invited man was to bring a guest – whether it was husband, partner, boy, slave... Full Leather for tops was the dress code. To add a bit of mystery, every man was to come hooded. And bring his cadre of toys. Boys and slaves were to be dressed in jocks, boots, gloves, and hooded.

The bar and boxes of cigars were laid out upstairs. Once a man retrieved those items, he hurried downstairs to what had become Drew's pleasure dungeon. Drew had made many trips to a local home improvement store and brought home quantities of lumber and chains, snaps, clips, hooks, et al. He had built himself a very handsome play space with four St. Andrew's crosses, three fuck tables, several racks, and whipping posts. The space was additionally outfitted with plenty of mirrors. Cameras were installed so you could watch your own fuck scene on several screens.

Early in the afternoon, Drew suited up. His cock was already bulging at the prospect of seeing horny men and boys in action. He added his favored floggers to the D ring of his chaps. Drew checked his watch and noted that his slave lawson was late – on the fucking day that there was so much to do. He would have his hide spanked for this transgression. Drew lighted a cigar without benefit of having his slave clip it or light it.

As he took several deep draws on the cigar, lawson appeared at the back door. He knelt on the doormat and bowed his head. He knocked softly on the door.

Drew pulled the door open and roughly pulled his slave in by the neck.

"What the fuck is your excuse?" Drew questioned as he pulled his meanest flogger off his D ring and laid several lashes across the handsome slave's back.

"I'm sorry, Master," lawson apologized, "there was an accident on the freeway and slave got tied up in traffic."

"It won't be the only tying up that will be done," Drew angrily said, as he backhanded the boy, "Hurry upstairs and undress. We have lots to do before the men arrive."

lawson scurried upstairs and returned shortly thereafter in boots, slave collar, and hood. He was already wearing the chastity cover over his cock and balls.

"That's better, slave. Now, get your ass over to the kitchen and get the snacks prepped. Pull out the tub from underneath the sink for ice...." The orders continued, but lawson was used to preparing items from the kitchen and hurriedly pulled the snacks and hors d'oeuvres from the cupboards and refrigerator.

As he carried trays upstairs, his Master swatted him on the ass. lawson respectfully replied, "Thank you, Master."

An hour later, the first of the Leathermen arrived.

Steve was the first to arrive – one of Drew's oldest friends. A top through and through. He brought with him a new pup – slender, hairless, but a handsome ass that just cried out for exploration. It would be. Led on a leash attached to his collar, Steve motioned for the boy to fall to his knees.

"Lick the host's boots, boy. Show your respect," Steve growled as he lashed the pup's back with the Leather strap of the leash.

The boy sank to his knees as he began licking Drew's boots. The two comrades watched for a few minutes.

"Your training is progressing well, Steve."

"Yeah, not fucking bad for three weeks, huh?" Steve replied as he lashed the boy several more times.

The boy was doing a decent job of licking. lawson, Drew's slave, appeared in the doorway and fell to his knees. He began licking Steve's boots as a symbol of his submission and servitude. Steve placed his right booted foot on the slave's back and pushed him to the ground, "On your fucking belly, slave," Steve ordered. lawson sprawled in the hallway and gave Steve's boots an excellent tonguing.

Steve pulled on his slaveboy's leash, "You could take lessons from this slaveboy. He knows how to worship a Leatherman's boots."

After a period, Drew yanked lawson's collar, "Up, slave. More work to do. Get the Leatherman a drink... Steve, what's your poison?"

lawson hurried upstairs and brought Steve his favored Black Martin. Only Steve and Drew's slave knew the precise ingredients, but it was heavily laced with rum.

"What cigar are you smoking these days, bro?"

"Brought my own this time, trying a new brand." Steve pulled out a large ring cigar and handed it to his slave. The slave carefully clipped it with Steve's clip and then presented it to his Master. He fucked up by not having matches, which should have been stowed in his boot. He received several hard slaps from Steve. lawson presented matches to the slave and the slave shakily lighted the match and lighted his man's cigar.

The Leathermen stoked their cigars and chatted for a few minutes until the door burst open, revealing Teddy. Even though hooded, there was no mistaking Teddy.

Teddy was a muscleman. Big fucking pecs and even bigger biceps. Teddy was definitely proud of his body and liked to show it off. It was no surprise that he wore no shirt. Chaps but no jock. His cock was swinging free. Wescos buckled at the thigh. Tight Damascus gloves. He rode his cycle that way, basically telling the world to fuck off if they didn't like what they saw.

"Hey, you horny fuckers. Let's get this fucking party started," he bellowed as he slapped Drew and Steve on the back.

His slave, another muscle stud, followed closely with Teddy's Leather bag of toys. The slave was wearing chaps and knee-high boots. Gloves.

Slave collar. No mistaking Teddy's slave. He had 'Property of Teddy' tattooed above his right nipple. They had been together for years – met in a weightlifting competition, which Teddy, of course, had won. Not only took home a trophy that night, but his future fuckboy as well. Drew couldn't remember the slave's name – that was how long he had simply known the slave as Teddy's property.

Teddy was self-assured, extremely arrogant about his alpha role in life, but was a helluva nice guy when he was your friend. And a helluva partier. He would keep the action going.

lawson dropped to his knees and began licking Teddy's boots.

Teddy kicked him away. "Get me a cigar, boy."

lawson obliged and after rotating the cigar for an even smoke, Teddy escorted his slave downstairs to restrain him in one of the slings. He always liked to have the sling that was front and center.

A cluster of guys arrived and the Leatherman and his slave were kept busy with greeting the men, swatting the slaves, offering cigars, and licking boots. All the men, including Steve and his slave, hustled downstairs to the dungeon to get a good 'station'. Yes, the party was going to be lively and filled with non-stop Leather sex. Drew liked it that way.

Morris and Hank arrived with their boy jim. Morris and Hank were two cops, known for their adventures with tough punks they had arrested and taken to their dungeon before turning the punks over to the authorities. They greeted Drew warmly. They were still in their tight blue uniforms and knee high Dehner boots.

"Hey, Drew," Hank said, with a shit-eating grin, "got a little bonus in the trunk. Thought the men would like some fresh meat to fuck."

"Hell, bring him in," Drew said, returning the grin, "You horny fucks." While jim clipped their cigars and fixed their drinks, Hank and Mo retrieved the bad boy from the trunk. He was a young, muscular punk – hooded with heavy duct-tape wrapped around his ankles and wrists. His chest was heaving underneath a wife beater tee shirt.

He struggled as the men escorted him up the porch and through the back door. jim retrieved the men's bag of toys and the four retreated to the basement. The boy was manacled to one of the remaining St. Andrew's crosses, facing toward the cross, and his pants lowered. Several of the Leathermen rubbed their cock-bulges. The phrases, "I want to fist that", "I want to plow it with my spade..." were heard. His ass was what men would term a 'bubble butt" and soon that bubble would burst and be leaking Leatherman's cum.

Within a few minutes, the party was in full swing with the sounds of Leather straps connecting with ass and dickmeat. Tits were pulled. Cocks and balls were twisted. Groans and moans and a couple of anguished cries. More tops with their boys or slaves arrived.

Drew smiled broadly as he surveyed the scene. The scene became even livelier when Drew smacked lawson's ass with a powerful paddle.

"Okay, men, you know the drill," Drew yelled, "change partners. Do-si-do."

Teddy was the only man to complain as he enjoyed working over his slave. He did not like to relinquish that role, but somewhat reluctantly went over to the twisting fresh meat on the St. Andrew's Cross.

He gripped the boy's neck with one of his iron fists. "Hold still, fucker. You need a good lashing." Teddy pulled a huge flogger off his belt and whipped the boy without stopping as the boy twisted and turned, attempting to avoid the Leather tails.

Teddy slammed his body against the boy, and whispered harshly, "I said hold still, you fucking piece of shit." The boy's tee shirt was soaked with sweat. Teddy simply ripped it off the boy's body and discarded it on the floor. It must have scared the boy as he stood still momentarily. The lashing continued.

Most of the men were too busy with their own S&M pleasuring to notice Teddy's treatment, but Hank and Mo caught each other's eyes and winked at one another. Mo thought, 'The bitch is getting what he deserves.' The boy had terrorized an old lady in the supermarket, snatching her purse and running toward the exit. Unfortunately, for him, Mo and Hank were entering the store just as he attempted his escape and caught him. Gripping him tightly, they escorted him back to the old lady and made him give her back her purse. They forced him down on his knees and made him apologize to her.

"Don't worry, ma'am," Hank said politely, "he'll get the punishment he deserves." Nobody seemed to notice as the two men lifted the punk into the trunk of the patrol car and drove away. Their initial thought of getting a couple of six packs for the party seemed irrelevant as they reasoned that a fresh fuck was much more appropriate. And with this crowd, he would be worked over... again and again.

Drew relished the role as the MASTER of the dungeon and MASTER of Ceremonies. He paddled whatever slave's ass he was working over and yelled 'Do-si-do' each time a switch was to be done.

After five rotations, the slave's asses were marked with the hash marks of floggers and paddles. The boys' tits and holes ached from the concentrated action. After a while, the Masters simply pulled off their cods, leaving their dripping cocks exposed. Hell, why bother to put your dick back in your cod when it was gonna be sucked or stuck up a boy's mineshaft. The dungeon exuded a rich smell of Leather, cigar smoke, and drying cum. A pity that there wasn't a Leather artist to capture the scene on canvas, a Leather orgy in full progress. Hooded men in black Leather pleasuring themselves with the willingness (or unwillingness) of handsome, naked boys.

After a time, Drew called an intermission of sorts and the Leather Masters retreated to the enclosed backyard of Drew's house. Fresh cigars were lighted and lawson was temporarily freed to bring drinks to the men. Spirited conversations and more spirited play among the Daddies ensued. The slaves and submissives remained in the dungeon, restrained to the slings, crosses, benches, and posts.

Drew stood back for a moment, reflecting on the success of the party. He was damned grateful to be a Man of Leather, proud of his sadistic tendencies. Proud of his Leatherhood.

Proud of his Leather Brothers. Temporarily housed in its cod, his Leathercock bulged with pride.

"Okay, Leathermen," Drew bellowed, "this party isn't over. Session #2! 'Do-Si-Do'" as the men rushed back downstairs to resume their activities. Let the fucking orgy continue.

THE TASKMASTER

The Taskmaster stood in the middle of the field. He wore a military cap which shaded his eyes. Squared, with a bill. Even though he had started the day in a tan tee shirt and military fatigue pants, he had removed the shirt as the sun rose in the sky. His muscular chest was coated in sweat. Each nipple had a gold ring in it. His cap and his pants were made out of Leather, but were made to resemble camouflage. His military boots were spit-shined, the top of his pants neatly tucked into the top of the boots. He wore black Leather wrist bands and he carried a single-tail whip, capable of inflicting great pain on the five boys under his supervision. It wasn't a surprise to learn that he was ex-military. His carefully-shaven head and the lack of a smile were further evidence. He smoked on a long, black cigar as he surveyed the boys at work.

Butch had been sent to the camp only three days before and had already been lashed twice by the Taskmaster. The red, bloody tracks on his back were evidence.

Butch was street-tough. Grown up on the streets of L.A., had joined a gang by the time he was fourteen and had dropped out of school.

"Don't need no fuckin' school," Butch thought, as he pledged with his blood. The gang had accepted him; he was big and beefy and could fuck almost anyone with his fists. He had already been in jail twice, when he stood before the Judge.

As the Judge pronounced sentence on Butch, Butch quietly unzipped his pants and sent a stream of piss against the Judge's bench.

He was led out of court, shouting obscenities. Handcuffed and ankle restraints were added as he was thrown into the bus that would take him to the camp. It was in the middle of nowhere. Chances of escape were slim, and even if an inmate did, he was at least forty miles from anywhere.

Butch arrived at the camp and was escorted by two brawny guards to a holding cell.

Against his protest, he was stripped of his clothes and held down while each body cavity was searched. Butch knew the guards were enjoying it – their doubled, gloved fists remained up his ass and down his throat longer than necessary. A small amount of weed, carefully sealed in plastic, was extracted from his asshole and a stiletto was removed from the inside of his boot.

He was given a pair of Leather shorts with a glory hole for his cock and balls to hang out and the ass cut out. Made it easier for examinations and punishment. A pair of boots and socks were issued to him as well. His head was shaved although he was allowed to keep his goatee. He was escorted to a cell. Four other inmates were housed in separate cells. Only half an hour after Butch arrived, the guards came in and motioned for all five to exit their cells and stand in the center of the room. They were told to stand at attention when the Taskmaster walked in. He carried his whip on his right hip. In his military fatigues and his cap pulled low over his eyes, he was an intimidating sight.

As he bellowed his orders to the boys, Butch's mind wandered. "I can take him," Butch thought, "given the chance. I can beat him."

"INMATE THREE," the Taskmaster bellowed, "REPEAT WHAT I JUST SAID!"

Butch sputtered an answer which was incorrect.

A silent nod from the Taskmaster was sent to the two guards, who roughly pulled Butch out of line and quickly secured him to a post in the room. The Taskmaster pulled the bullwhip off his belt and proceeded to lash Butch's back. Five ugly lines of blood quickly appeared on Butch's back. He cried out as the third hit his back.

Infractions were plentiful and soon all the boys had similar blood tracks on their backs.

"NEXT TIME IT WILL BE YOUR COCKS!" the Taskmaster informed them. He had the boys' full attention after that.

Butch survived the next two days without further incident. On the next morning, however, he was working in the field, planting seedlings for the farm. All the profits belonged to the farm owner, a sadistic Leather Master who ruled with a Leather fist. Seldom seen, but his presence could be felt. It was back breaking work – bending over, planting those damn seedlings six inches apart in rows which stretched to the horizon. Butch stretched his back. The Taskmaster was standing twenty-five feet away. Butch couldn't help but notice that the Taskmaster had unzipped his fatigues and was holding his sizable cock in his hand. Playing with it, massaging his low hangers as well.

Butch's gaze must have lasted a second too long, because the Taskmaster began striding toward him. Butch quickly bent back down and was mounding the dirt around the seedling when two booted feet appeared within his sight.

He looked up; viewing first the Taskmaster's cock standing erect and then the cold glint of the Taskmaster's eyes. They were soulless.

"You lookin' at somethin', boy?"

"No, Sir."

"The hell you weren't, boy. I saw you looking at my cock..."

"No, Sir, I was just stretching..." Butch explained as he lifted his eyes to meet the Taskmaster's.

With that a steady stream of piss hit Butch squarely in the face.

"Drink it, pussy boy. Taste your Taskmaster's piss."

Butch resisted which resulted in the whip to be unfurled and it caught Butch squarely on the back, reopening one of the bloody tracks from the first day.

The Taskmaster ordered him to stand and turn around. Butch received five more lashes, reopening all the tracks and creating a fresh one.

"Turn around."

Butch obliged, only to see the Taskmaster shaking his cock to release the drops of piss that remained.

"Don't let it happen again, boy," the Taskmaster warned as he marched back to his central location.

Butch glared after the Taskmaster but returned to his work before he would be cited for another infraction.

Even though the boys were separated in individual cells there were moments when they exchanged low, whispered conversations. Even though the guards were supposed to act as sentries within the cellblock, they often snuck away for a smoke or fuck breaks. The guards routinely charged in and abused one or another of the boys. The boys were routinely sodomized while held down by two or three guards. You could try to fight back, but hell, you were outnumbered. It created a brotherhood of sorts among the inmates. Of course, they all wanted revenge on the Taskmaster but there didn't seem to be much opportunity. Only one remained silent most of the time. A big, burly black man named 'Charlie'. Charlie had received his share of lashings. His back was covered with dried, bloody marks from the repeated lashings. He was heavily muscled and had several ugly scars near his right cheek and on his neck.

One night, Butch whispered to Charlie, "Hey, man, how did you get those scars?"

"None of your fuckin' business," was Charlie's reply. The conversation ended.

A week had passed and all the inmates were dirty, covered in blood, dirt, and dried sweat.

Sunrise and the guards came streaming in to retrieve the 'field hands'. The inmates rose hastily as their bodies were lashed with the Taskmaster's whip. He was dressed in his military fatigues, already chomping on a cigar.

The inmates were hastened out into a field to the south of the building and were given flats of yet more seedlings to plant.

Despite the lashings, Butch was beginning to respond to the conditioning. His back no longer ached as it had on the first several days. The sun didn't seem to bother him as much as he began to plant the endless row of plants.

Charlie was about fifteen rows ahead of Butch. His big beefy hands did not grasp the seedlings as well as the others. He had dropped quite a few and pounded them under his feet – destroying the evidence.

Out of the corner of his eye, Butch saw Charlie pick up a sharpened rock and put in the top of his boot. "Trouble, oh shit," thought Butch, but minding your own business was one thing he had learned.

Charlie stood up to stretch and the Taskmaster came marching toward Charlie, whip unfurled.

As the Taskmaster drew his right hand back with the whip, Charlie caught the whip and jerked it toward him. He kneed the Taskmaster in the groin, giving him time to extract the sharpened rock from his boot. He went for the Taskmaster's throat. Even from fifteen rows away, Butch could see a line of blood appear.

"What do I do?" Butch thought, "do I join in? Or do I continue planting?"

He wisely chose the latter as five guards came running toward the endangered Taskmaster.

Charlie was quickly subdued and spread-eagled on the dirt, held down by three of the guards while the other two kicked him with their military boots. By this time, the Taskmaster was mopping his neck with his tee shirt. He brought down the whip repeatedly on Charlie's bruised and bloodied back. A number of racial epithets filled the air, as the guards continued to kick Charlie and then spit on him.

They dragged him away by his feet.

After the four remaining inmates were fed, they were lined up and marched out into the courtyard. Charlie was spread-eagled on a wooden cross, his arms and legs tied into place with rough rope. It had already cut into Charlie's flesh. Charlie was naked.

The Taskmaster was in his Leather fatigues, his boots gleaming in the late afternoon sun.

His cock was hanging out of his pants, fully erect.

"I'm gonna teach you boys a lesson that may cut short any plans on revenge against me or the guards," the Taskmaster bellowed. With that he put on a pair of tight, black gloves and unfurled his whip. With one hand massaging his already tumescent cock, he expertly landed the whip on the tip of Charlie's cock.

Charlie screamed in pain as the whip connected for a second and third time. The fourth and fifth were an underhanded flicking which caught each one of Charlie's balls. A second rotation and Charlie was twisting and turning, flinching, screaming.

The Taskmaster marched around to the other side and proceeded to lash Charlie's back and ass with thirty hard lashes.

After he had finished, the Taskmaster returned to face Charlie. Drawing close to Charlie's face, he hissed, "Next time you better finish the job."

The next day, Charlie's cell was empty.

As the boys marched to the field, they saw that Charlie had been tied down to four stakes in the middle of the courtyard. He would remain there all day, as the temperature rose to 102 degrees. The guards checked on him occasionally, spitting or pissing on him and laughing. Charlie remained silent – he had a Leather glove stuffed in his mouth.

Finally at the end of the day, Butch saw them carry Charlie away. For days, the inmates didn't know if he had survived, if he had been transported elsewhere or what. No one spoke of him.

About two weeks later, the inmates were hustled out of bed. Another day of planting those damned seedlings. Butch was feeling okay that morning as he had not created any problems and had not been lashed in a week. His body was strengthening and he actually was looking forward to the physical work.

The guards ordered them to attention for their daily inspection.

In came the Taskmaster, but it was not the one they were accustomed to. It was Charlie in full fatigues. Leather cap and Leather spit-shined boots. Charlie had become one of them. He bellowed, "ALL RIGHT, YOU PUSSY BOYS. YOU'VE HAD IT EASY WITH THE PREVIOUS TASKMASTER. AIN'T GONNA BE THAT WAY NO MORE, YOU BUNCH OF ASSHOLES. WE'RE GOING TO STEP UP PRODUCTION OR YOU'RE GONNA GET YOUR LILY-WHITE ASSES WHIPPED BY ME." And as the day progressed, it was apparent that he was a meaner muthafucker than the last. Butch got lashed three times, not knowing what the infractions were. His body was crisscrossed with bloodied tracks of welts. His cock hurt like hell as the tip of the single tail had caught it more than once. He lay in bed exhausted, aching, ready for revenge.

He thought of the brief attempt to befriend Charlie. Anger boiled over as he silently slipped out of bed. The guards were off somewhere, apparently pleasuring themselves.

Butch stole through the camp, until he found the Taskmaster's hut. Entering as quietly as possible, he could hear Charlie's loud snoring.

Charlie's military belt hung on the chair of his desk. Pulling out the knife from the belt's sheath, he leapt on top of Charlie and started slashing.

Charlie woke from his sleep and quickly had Butch's arms pinned behind his back. Handcuffs came out from the desk drawer as Charlie manacled Butch to the bed frame.

Without ceremony, Charlie pulled down Butch's military briefs and plunged his substantial dick into Butch's hole. Butch's scream was quickly muffled by Charlie's huge hand as he pumped his muscular dick into Butch. His huge load of cum spilled out of Butch's raped hole as Charlie slapped his ass repeatedly.

He dragged Butch out of the hut and spread-eagled him in the compound center. Butch lay there in pain the rest of the night.

And he lay there as the inmates were brought out to witness his continued abuse. The guards kicked him and pissed on him. As the day progressed, the sun beat mercilessly down on his aching body. The cum had dried in his asshole and the guard's piss stung every welt and bloodied mark. Butch was lapsing in and out of reality as he was finally released at sundown. He was taken to the recovery center. The former Taskmaster and Charlie were both there to supervise. And for the next three or four days, Butch was subjected to an unceasing barrage of verbal humiliation and continued whipping and beatings. Everybody wanted to gut punch him, kick him in the balls, spit on him, piss on him. The former Taskmaster spent a lot of time with him; apparently this was his new assignment.

Butch was hardened when he came and was stronger because of the physical workouts he had endured, but this was pure hell. He kept wishing that he would just die. He had given up hope of surviving, or of escaping the brutality at the hands of all these men.

On the fifth day, Butch woke after a fitful night in which he lapsed between sleep and waking from the torturing he had been subjected to. He woke to find himself tightly bound to a wooden chair in a cavernous building. Arms wrenched behind him, ankles tightly tied to the legs of the chair. A gag in his mouth. He wrestled only momentarily before he realized that there was not a chance of escape. He continued to wish he would just die. Far off in the distance, he heard a door slam and the sound of military boots marching closer and closer to him. The door to the room was opened and six men walked in, led by an imposing figure. He wore military fatigues tucked neatly into his boots. His massive chest was bare, with the exception of the dog tags around his neck and silver nipple rings. Silver armbands around his muscular arms and Leather gauntlets covered his hands. He wore a military cap, pulled low over his forehead. He carried a furled black single tail whip. Flakes of dried blood appeared on it. The man looked familiar, but Butch couldn't quite rationalize who he was.

"Well, inmate, you have proven to be a real troublemaker, a fuck-up, which we don't tolerate...," the man began. The five men stood in back of him, their faces impassive as the man continued the long litany of transgressions against Butch. He was certain that he was going to be disposed of. He struggled momentarily, causing the man to interrupt his own speech.

"Try all you want, shithead, you can't get out of those ropes. I tied them myself. Go ahead try...." The man folded his arms and leaned against the nearby table. He started laughing and the other men joined in.

Butch merely lowered his head and remained silent.

The man continued his sentencing. Butch ceased listening. He knew he was going to die.

Finally, the man approached Butch. Butch eyed him wearily, assuming that the man would pull out a gun and shoot him at any moment. He closed his eyes.

"OPEN YOUR EYES, PUSSY BOY!" the man ordered.

Butch's eyes flew open, in time to see the man unzip his pants and aim his large cock at Butch's face. A spray of piss assaulted Butch's face and swept up and down his body.

"That's for pissing on my bench." The man was the Judge who had ordered Butch to the camp in the first place.

Butch still waited for gun fire to rip through his body. Or an attack with knives. Or someone choking him. None of those came. Instead, the men silently filed out. Only the Judge remained. He untied the ropes.

"Inmate, stand at attention," the Judge barked. Butch made an attempt to stand, but his knees buckled. The Judge caught him in his arms before Butch fell to the floor. The Judge slammed him against the closest wall and held Butch around the neck with his big meaty hand.

Butch prepared himself for a gut punch or a kick to the balls as best he could, but he was just too weakened.

"Prisoner, you have proven a difficult subject, not eligible to re-enter society." the Judge droned on, but Butch was only aware of words and phrases of his 'fucking up.' "However...," the Judge paused, "The administration feels that you would make an excellent Taskmaster..."

"Whaat?" Butch replied, still in a weakened state.

"You have advanced to the next stage and will become a Taskmaster here at my farm." The Judge was the Leather Master who ruled with a Leather fist.

With that, the Judge took the prisoner down and led Butch to his own Taskmaster hut. A plateful of food and jugs of water stood on a table. Leather military fatigues, black military boots, and a Leather cap were laid carefully on the bed.

"Now, get some rest... we have fresh inmates coming next week and they are yours to supervise. I know a good man for the job when I see one," the Judge concluded, "I've become very wealthy sentencing tough boys like you to work on my farms and you are going to make me even wealthier." His Leather fist grabbed Butch's cock and balls, pulling on them hard, "And don't you fucking forget who your Leather Master is."

With that the Judge closed the door behind him, leaving Butch alone.

When the inmates arrived, a man in military fatigue pants stood nearby, eyeing them. His furled single tail whip was in his gloved right hand, ready to inflict discipline. He was shirtless, revealing his muscular torso.

The Taskmaster accompanied the recruits out to the field, where there were flats of seedlings to plant.

As he applied his whip to the back of one of the recruits, he rubbed his crotch.

"Damn, I'm gonna like this job," Butch thought.

THE DEVIL'S DEN

As he entered the bedroom, Terry began to unbutton his shirt. His whole body ached after a rigorous day at work. His right shoulder caught as he began to remove his shirt. 'Damn,' he thought, 'I may have really injured it with that last fucker'. He had been in pursuit of a lowlife drug dealer when he slipped in the alley and landed on the shoulder. Man against concrete, not a good mix. As he removed the shirt, a huge bruise – black and blue revealed itself. 'Shit', he muttered, as he tenderly rubbed it. He grimaced as he removed the shirt and stood for several minutes, rubbing it and massaging it.

After taking off the rest of his uniform, he stood in silently reverie as he examined the rest of his body in the mirror.

'Not bad-looking for a forty-nine year old fucker like me'. He absently played with his cock and balls as he headed into the bathroom and turned on the hot water in the shower. He stood with his hands plastered against the wall, the water streaming down his face and coursing down his handsome body.

The hot water released some of the tenseness as he continued to rotate the shoulder. At least there was nothing broken.

As he relaxed, his thoughts replayed the pursuit. The boy was probably 25-27 years old. Slim – tight white wife beater tee shirt and packed jeans – holes in both knees. A healthy crop of hair under each pit and on top of his head. A rim beard and thin black mustache. Brown eyes – he had noted them as the boy turned briefly to see how far away the cop was from him. As Terry made a grab for the boy's shoulder, he had slipped and the perp had gotten away.

'Wonder what was in those jeans?' Terry considered, not worried about the pot or drug paraphernalia he might find. He wanted to grab the boy's cock and balls.

His cock was responding to the possibilities and Terry lost interest in his sore shoulder and began massaging his hardening cock.

'Damn, wish I had caught him…' Terry mused, 'he would have been my captive faggot-boy for the night.'

Terry was a twenty-four year veteran of the police force and a thirty year veteran of the Leather Brotherhood. He liked to play in gear. He belonged to a small group of cops who were also Leathermen. They knew each other. They protected each other's interests in S&M, as it was condemned by the police force and the public at large.

"If the public only knew how many bad boys we have punished and administered our own justice to, they would thank us," he sighed and finally concluded, "although, maybe not."

He turned off the water and headed back into the bedroom.

Pulling open the closet door, he selected his favorite uniform – black Leather. Shirt, cycle jacket, and pants. He pulled on his patrol boots. Retrieving his gloves and Muir cap, he went downstairs and hastily prepared his evening meal. Even though he was hurting, he needed to unwind. He needed to be among his own kind. He chowed down the meal and grabbing his keys and helmet, he mounted his cycle and headed for 'The Stud Farm', a private men's club for men of his persuasion. Most of the Leather cops had a membership there.

He arrived ten minutes later and after keying in his code, opened the door, and marched up the steps to the club's bar.

Don, Frank and Scott were already there, similarly dressed in head-to-toe Leather. Drinks in hand. Cigars being stoked.

The guys quickly fell into conversation about the events of the day.

Frank quickly announced that he had captured the punk he had been pursuing after the punk had robbed an old lady with nothing more than a comb in his hoodie pocket.

"Want to see him?" Frank said, as he tucked his gloved hands into his belt.

"Don't tell me...," Scott started, but was interrupted by Frank.

"Yep, I have him in the downstairs tank."

The four Leathermen marched down to the basement where there was a fully-equipped dungeon for the pleasure of the members.

It was dimly lighted, but the guys could make out a naked boy strapped to the St. Andrew's Cross in the recesses of the dungeon.

The men hooted as they rushed to get a closer look.

Gloved hands were soon slapping the boy's asscheeks, squeezing his cock, pulling on his nips. The boy was hooded with a black Leather hood, a plug in his mouth, a blindfold over his eyes.

All four men jockeyed for position, but Frank had captured him and had the right to subject the boy to his initial manhandling.

Frank pulled the boy's head back and yelled, "Listen, you lowlife punk, you're going to receive a little rough justice by a group of hard-fucking men. You won't rob any more old ladies or else, you'll be back for a return visit."

With that Frank slapped the boy's face. The boy moaned despite the protection of the Leather hood.

Each man took his turn slowly – paddling the boy's ass until it had ridges of welts, flogging the boy's shoulders and back until they were similarly patterned. Plugging his ass with dildos. Applying clothespins in an arched pattern down the boy's ribcage. On the boy's dick, and balls, and on his nips. The boy twisted and turned, but it was to no avail. He would not escape the tight bondage he found himself in.

Finally, it was Terry's turn. He pulled the flogger off his belt and began administering his own form of justice to the victim. Despite the pain in his shoulder, the flogging rotations seemed to loosen the shoulder. The harder he struck, the better it felt.

And once Terry got started he did not want to stop. All of the shit of the day translated into a series of flogs and paddles to the abused lowlife.

"Damn, I needed that..." as he wiped the sweat from his forehead.

Footsteps were heard on the stairs.

"Hey, fuckers! Heard you had a pussy boy down here." a voice said. It was Captain Mick, their Departmental superior.

He was a big fucker – size 13 EE boots. Broad frame, big chest. He puffed on his cigar as he marched toward the circle of men.

"Yep, Captain, we just gave him a little rough justice."

The Captain marched up to the boy and slapped him hard across the face.

"Nice work, men. What do you think – I don't think we'll have any more trouble out of him," as the Captain hauled off and slapped the boy's ass a number of times. He puffed on his cigar before squeezing the boy's balls. The boy flinched. Pulling a braided flogger off his belt, Captain Mick lashed the boy until he drew blood. Captain Mick just laughed as he turned to his men.

"Gotta haul ass men, got my own cunt boy to take care of at home," as he marched up the steps and disappeared.

Don whispered, "I'm glad he is one of us, but I've always felt uncomfortable around Mick. I know he's a fellow sadist, but..." The thought was left unfinished as Captain Mick strode back down into the dungeon. "This might loosen the boy up... or tighten him up," he said, as he chortled at his own joke. He jammed a rubber plug up the boy's ass. The boy twisted and moaned as Mick jammed it further up the boy's abused hole. He held the boy by the neck, "And don't let it fucking fall out, or you'll have me to answer to." Mick disappeared once again.

"Come on, bro, let's go upstairs and let the scumfaggot think about the beatings he just got," Don suggested.

The men trooped upstairs and settled in the smoking lounge, thick with smoke and filled with men.

The conversation, of course, quickly turned to their occupation and the challenges faced. And Captain Mick.

They concluded that Mick was one of them, even more sadistic than they were.

Terry filled them in on his misfortune.

"What does that boy look like?" asked Scott.

Terry described the perp.

"Oh, yeah, I think I know who you mean... I arrested him last summer. Had him here. We worked him over, don't you remember?" Don insisted.

Terry had no recollection, but hell; they had abused quite a few boys in the dungeon since last summer.

"I remember him because he has a pentagram tattooed on his dick."

"A Satan worshipper?" Terry asked.

"Well, if he isn't, it's a hell of a birthmark," Don countered.

The conversation led to a discussion of a supposed coven of Satanic worshippers that had set up shop in the county. Their meetings were at an undetermined place, but some of the rituals sounded intriguing to the men. Naked male flesh being used and abused.

"Hmmm," mused Terry, "maybe we should find out more about it."

The men reconvened in the dungeon where they each did a second rotation on the faggotscum on the cross. The boy's ass was clenched tightly around the rubber plug. He was apparently concentrating on keeping it in his hole as the floggings on his reddened ass continued. The men continued but Terry's shoulder was really aching and so, he excused himself and went home.

The next day at headquarters was usual – a list of overnight occurrences that needed investigation and Terry, despite his aching shoulder, was back on duty.

He reported on the escape of the lowlife who had evaded his capture. The perp had apparently held up a drug store and had gotten away with a couple of hundred dollars. It riled Terry that he had not put a stop to the punk as he rubbed his shoulder and assured Captain Mick that he would seek out the perpetrator. He mounted his cycle. He went to interview the drug store manager who was terrified that the creep would strike again. Terry assured the nervous manager that he was on the prowl for the lowlife. He would get his man. However, by the end of the day, he had achieved no success in capturing the punk, and so, Terry headed home.

He retreated to his bedroom and slipped on his comfortable Leathers. He wolfed down a quick dinner, but was too anxious to sit and watch TV. Retrieving his cycle jacket, gauntlets and helmet, he mounted his cycle and headed out. He cruised the streets looking for the punk. He was headed straight out of the downtown area, when he spotted a young boy walking hastily. Head bowed, a hoodie covering his features. What caught his attention was a spray-painted pentagram on the back of the jacket.

He slowed up and parked his cycle in an alley. Following on foot, the boy continued walking hastily. Terry took long strides to keep up, but at the same time had to remain a far enough distance so that the boy would not know he was being followed. The boy never looked back, just continuing on his march. Finally, he turned to the right and disappeared into the night.

As Terry approached the intersection, he looked up at the road sign. "Cemetery Ridge Road."

"Fuck," thought Terry, "I'll bet that's where they meet." He returned to his cycle. He called Scott on his cellphone.

"Scott, you feel like a little adventure tonight?" Scott was at 'The Stud Farm' with Don and Frank.

"Rock and roll," was the collective response, but the three wanted to go home and exchange their uniforms for their heavy cycle Leathers.

About a half hour later, the four men had congregated near Terry's cycle. Each carried necessary equipment on their cycle jacket belts for any trouble they might encounter.

The four men walked up 'Cemetery Ridge Road', silently observing the surroundings and on high alert for any unusual activity.

As they neared the entrance to the cemetery, they all put on black Leather hoods and drew the knives which were clipped to their belts. This would be a tough crowd, no doubt.

All was quiet – only the chirping of crickets was heard. Even the crickets stopped chirping as the men fanned out in pairs and marched silently into the cemetery.

The moon was obscured by a heavy cloud cover; however, the tombstones seemed to be eerily glowing in the dark.

"Shit," Terry began in whispered tones, "I don't see anything..." as Don grabbed his sleeve, "Over there, I see lights..." And it was true, there were lights coming from behind a grove of trees. Terry quietly radioed the other two and gave them approximate bearings. The four men reunited on the ridge, which overlooked a small hollow.

They were hidden by the bushes that had grown up surrounding the ridge and could observe the goings on.

A circle of half-naked men, most of them of slender build, surrounded a large table-like tombstone. Terry counted five young men in the circle. The sixth, a young, naked man was lying on top of it. Candles surrounded his body. The men were walking around the 'table' and appeared to be dripping wax from the candles on to the boy's body. They were chanting. One man stood at the head of the 'table'. He was wearing a black hood, similar to the hoods worn by the witness cops. He was leading the chanting.

As the men continued to watch, they took in more details. The men all had pentagrams crudely drawn on their chests. Only the naked man on the table was without one.

"Must be an induction ritual," whispered Don.

"Let's regroup and discuss this at the club," suggested Frank. The four left quietly, unobserved, and reconvened at the club.

The hour was late when they arrived back at the club, but all were anxious to talk about it. They talked until 2 AM. The club never closed, but the men had duties to perform the next day and so, went to their respective homes.

As Terry undressed, he rubbed his cock thoughtfully. As he crawled into bed, he couldn't stop thinking about what he had witnessed. What would he report? What would Don, Frank and Scott report the next day?

The next evening, Terry hurried home, suited up and headed for the 'Stud Farm.'

Terry secured a table in the smoker's lounge. He was puffing on a big, black cigar as the other men filtered in.

He opened the conversation, "Don't know about you fuckers, but that was hot... I wanted to run down and participate. Drip some wax on that naked boy's cock." The men were in full agreement. They had not revealed any of the details during Captain Mick's daily meeting with the whole department.

The conversation regressed into a review of hot wax scenes the men had individually participated in, until returning to a professional dialogue.

"Don't know if Satanic ritual is on the books as a crime.... they could say it's religious freedom to practice their rituals," Terry said.

"Trespassing, perhaps?" Don suggested.

"Exposing oneself, at least the boy on the table was..." Scott offered, "but that seems pretty lame."

"Drug use?" offered Frank, "but none of them ingested anything, at least not that I saw."

The men quietly returned several more times to the cemetery, always hooded, always in their heaviest Leathers. Knives drawn. But the ritual was apparently not taking place. On the fourth visit, however, six young men were congregated around the same table and a young, naked man was lying on the table. Once again, hot wax was slowly dripped on his body. The hooded man stood at the head of the table. The men took in the fact that he was extremely muscular. His hood had two horns projecting from the forehead. His chanting was mesmerizing and the boys seemed to increase their circlings at a faster clip as the man chanted faster and faster, whipping the boys into a frenzy. Their naked cocks were pulled out of their faded jeans. The four men continued to watch as each boy gathered something off the ground. The boys now wielded small single tail floggers. The boys lashed the naked man as they encircled the victim. Faster and faster, they circled around the table. The cop dicks were hardening in their respective Leathers, precum appearing in their piss slits. The four men silently wanted to take part in the beatings. With more information gathered, however, the four cops once again reconvened at the club.

"Man, that was fucking hot," Terry exclaimed and the three men nodded in agreement. They were all rubbing their crotches as they disappeared into the dungeon and wanked off.

On the following day at work, Terry got a break in the case he had been pursuing. The street punk had attempted to rob a liquor store, but the manager was a tough 'Nam vet. He kept a baseball bat behind the counter and clubbed the punk. Terry responded to the call and quickly arrested the boy. But instead of taking him to the headquarters, he threw the boy in the trunk of his patrol car. He discretely deposited him at the club before returning home and gearing up. This was gonna be fun as he suited up in his Leather cop uniform.

By the time he arrived at the club, the punk was trussed up against the St. Andrew's Cross.

He greeted the men with a broad grin on his face.

"Ah, Terry, you could never hide a secret. You must have gotten your man," as the four men placed black Leather executioner's hoods over their faces and trooped downstairs.

The boy was restrained, facing forward on the cross. And a collective 'Ah hah' issued forth as the four men witnessed a crude pentagram drawn on the boy's chest.

Interrogation ensued. The punk was silent, but not for long.

"Talk, boy," as Terry tightened his Leathered hand around the boy's balls and pulled.

Silence lasted only until Terry got right up in his face and hissed, "If you don't start talking, I'll pull these balls right off you, you fucking scum."

The boy finally started talking, revealing that the coven leader was their Master. The boys were his slaves. They were sent out to acquire money for the Master's needs, which included his strong cocaine habit. He had brainwashed them into believing that he was an emissary of Satan and controlled their destiny. Most of them were poorly educated and on the streets, he gave them a place to live and fed them. They were to bring new recruits to the coven with the promise of a better life. Apparently the Master's desire was to have a dozen converts, which would make him the unholy thirteenth.

The four cops reconvened upstairs after pleasuring themselves with the boy.

With the boy captured and restrained, there was one less boy to worry about.

The next night, the four cops, in their heavy Leathers and hoods returned to the cemetery. They were rewarded with a circle of light near the same location.

They calculated their plan of action as they crept closer to the circle.

Fanning out in pairs they made a wide circle around the grove. On each belt, a length of bondage rope was tied.

The boys were concentrating on their own cocks, rubbing them to fullness. The hooded Master had pulled his own cock out and was rubbing it with both his hands.

As the men inched nearer to the Master, they could hear him chanting, "I am an emissary of Satan. My seed is holy and precious to the Dark Lord."

The boys responded, "Your seed is superior, Master. Planting your seed in us is your desire."

The Master continued to rub his cock, "Through my seed, you will be powerful and strong like the Dark Lord and this emissary."

The boys responded, "Yes, Master, we are the repository…"

With that, the Master commanded them to lay their hands on the naked victim. As they did this, they unzipped their jeans and bent over, spreading their legs and asscheeks, their hands placed on the naked boy.

The cops knew what was coming next. The Master marched to the boy nearest to him on his left and began an intense ass fucking. His face constricted as his demon pole glided in the boy's stretched hole.

"Time for action, men," Terry announced. With that they rushed out into the circle, quickly restraining the Master's hands behind his back.

The boys did not move, not knowing if it was part of the ritual.

"DON'T MOVE!" commanded Scott to the boys as he held his knife to the Master's throat.

Terry unlaced the hood. A look of surprise appeared on the cops' faces. The Master was a cop who belonged to the 'Stud Farm'. Their own Captain Mick.

At the ritual, four men in black hoods chant the ritual as the half-naked boys respond with their chanting. A healthy young man was restrained on the table. However, the ceremony was not being held at the cemetery, it was being held at the club. The four hooded men were cops Scott, Frank, Don and Terry, interested in subjecting their initiates to S&M. And restrained to the St. Andrew's Cross, observing silently with a gag in his mouth, was Captain Mick. Sometimes cops take the law into their own hands, which are armed with floggers and paddles.

TRY IT: I THINK YOU'LL LIKE IT!

It was another typical weekend. I was suited up in my jock with the studded cod, chaps, butt paddle attached to the D ring of the chaps, Wesco crotch-highs, harness, vest, Muir cap and my new soft-as-butter gauntlets. My bag of toys rested near my booted feet. Ready for action. There was only one problem – the boy was apparently a 'no show'. Typical of boys. Make a commitment and show they have no balls by not showing up. Shit. I was hornier than hell. Needed to have some man-to-boy action. But I had waited patiently for him to show for over an hour and that was my indication that I would have to do some self-pleasuring. I marched across the property. There was an old stone wall that I liked to take a boy to, position him, and do some warm-ups on his ass. Boys are instructed to wear chaps so that when they take off their jeans, I'll have a nice, handsome ass to flog. Oh well.

I stood against the wall and massaged my cock in its cod while I lighted a cigar. My cock responded quickly to the massage, hard and firm in its cod. My mind absently wandered while massaging. What does it feel like to have this man's cod pressed against those ass cheeks?

I snapped off my cod and turned it inside out. Soon the spiked cod was pressing against my dickflesh. Pricking my prick with its sharp little points. As I drew deeply on the cigar, fuck, I realized it felt great. I gripped the cod tightly and began grinding the spikes into my erect cockshaft. I could feel my cock pulsating with the sensation. I reached up further and soon spikes were assaulting my cock's head. I could feel it enlarging, opening. Attempting to take one of the spikes in the piss-hole. Fuck, felt great.

I reached down and pressed the spikes into my firm ball sack. Oh, yeah.

A moan issued from my own throat as I continued to press the spikes against my manhood.

Pretty soon, both hands were working on that cod. I stopped momentarily to place my nipclamps on my nips. They were reserved for the boy, but hell, he wasn't here. They bit painfully into my man nips. My head arched back as the initial sting of the clamps introduced themselves to my nips.

I continued to press the spikes into my dickshaft. I could feel my bone throbbing with excitement.

I took the paddle off my D ring and began paddling my own ass, maintaining the steady massage of pricks against my cockshaft. Cock's head. Balls.

I willed my cock not to cum. No, I wanted to prolong this fuck session as long as I could.

I eased off and took several long drags of the cigar. Pulling on the chain which connected my clamps.

A throatier moan issued forth.

I spread my legs and straddled the stone wall. Touching my cod to the top of the stone wall, I began slowly rubbing the cod against the stone wall. The spikes ground into my dickshaft. Not as good as a boy's hole, but very erotic. Very stimulating.

I laid face down on the wall – it was just broad enough to accommodate my chest – my nips were now pressed tightly against the wall, the clamps pinching the hell out of them. I rubbed my cod back and forth. My cock was pulsing with the sadistic spikes pressing into my cockflesh.

Wish I had a boy to take some photos of this as I was, in essence, fucking the wall.

Damn, it felt so good as I slid my cod against the wall, pressing my nips tightly against it.

Another moan escaped my throat.

The cigar continued to burn, I now had a healthy ash, which I deposited in my own mouth. Tasted salty, just like my mancum would taste when I released my load.

I got back up and massaged my entire cod. Balls first, cockshaft, cock's head. Those gloves gripped each part of the equipment tightly, the spikes telling me that they were sadistic little fuckers. If they couldn't have a boy's ass to plow, they would sure as hell substitute my own man meat.

I pulled on the clamps. My nips were throbbing.

I paddled my ass a few more times before returning both gloved hands to my throbbing cod. My cock's head had escaped the cod, hard and glistening with precum.

I leaned against the wall and slowly unsnapped the cod. My cockflesh sprang forward, patterned with red pinpricks all over it.

My buttery soft gloves stroked it. I could feel the mancum gathering strength. I began stroking my cockshaft and pretty soon, of course, I shot a load of mancum. I kept cumming and cumming. I stood there for several minutes wiping the cum with my soft gauntlets. Pity I had no boy to share it with. But hell, you make do, or cum, with what you have! Try it; I think you'll like it.

ABOUT THE AUTHOR

G.W. Leatherman Parks has been a Leatherman for over thirty years. He is a proud member of the Leather Archives and Museum in Chicago and writes frequently for FLAGSHIP, the newsletter of Fits Like a Glove. He has also been published in *Drummer and Cuir: For LeatherMen by LeatherMen*. He is a collector of vintage Leather, Leather artwork and photography.

This is G.W. Leatherman Parks' sixth book. His first book *Leatherdaddy,* second book *Leather Nazis,* third book *A Harvest of G.O.L.D.: Leather Bikers on the Prowl,* fourth book *Packed Cod, Hard Rod*, and fifth book *Sadistic Leathercops* are available from Amazon.com, TheNazcaPlainsCorp.com or your local bookstore.